"Sex is not the answer. Sex is the question. *Yes* is the answer."
—Anonymous

For SAM

Foreword

It's happening again, the naughty stories are flowing! Those stories that never fail to delight and entertain—to teach you, O lucky reader, a whole lot more than just your basic alphabet.

We are now four volumes in to this popular erotica series and as these twenty-seven new stories prove (that's correct, there's one bonus story for that lucky letter 'K'), the wicked imaginations of your favorite erotica writers haven't let up. In my humble opinion, the stories just keep getting better. And by 'better' I mean raunchier, riskier, a little more challenging than just your ordinary naughty stories.

When Ms. Tyler first launched this series a few years back, it was hard to predict how each writer would define what a simple word like *naughty* really meant. Speaking as someone who's read, written, edited, and published a whole lot of erotica over the years, I am still in awe of how classy the writers in this particular series are when it comes to telling dirty stories; in awe of how far their imaginations are willing to go; to how many different places the word 'naughty' can take us. All we, as readers, have to do to take advantage of these tempting journeys is crack open the book to any page and start reading. Before you know it, you're hopping aboard some very sexy rides.

And don't let some old-fashioned notion of naughty fool you, either. Don't let it lull you into a false understanding of the word; that naughty somehow means nice, or cutesy, or feminine and harmless—just a mild indecency. A lot of these stories go out on a limb. Not just in their sexual daring or erotic exploits, but in the unexpectedly deep range of their emotions. I think that's what I like best about this series overall. You'll have some raunchy fun here, but you'll also see sides to some well-known writers that you won't see in other erotica collections.

Sound tempting? Are you ready to run the gamut of the complete erotic alphabet? Well then pick a letter, any letter, and hold on tight for the wild ride!

Marilyn Jaye Lewis
July 2005

Introduction

I'm a tease. I know it. I can't help it. Or maybe I don't *want* to help it. You can never be sure. That's how we teases operate. I've worked to perfect my teasing ability since high school, when I would gaze at an object of my affection, look away, and then look back again—just like in my favorite Massive Attack song.

The fact that I'm fairly shy by nature, that I have long dark bangs that tend to fall in front of my deep-brown eyes, that I am not one of the bold girls who stalks after what she wants...those points always seems to work in my favor. Because I *do* get what I want. Every single time. As do the lovers in this book.

In the following stories, men and women give over to their dirtiest desires, joining up in menages, dabbling in S&M, venturing into voyeurism and exhibitionism. Hosting a group of friends for a hockey night has never been so sexy as in Cate Robertson's "Game Night," listening to an oldies record while trying to decipher the lyrics creates super-charged sparks in Ayre Riley's "...and Leslie," and finding out where your lover (or your lover's lover) stands on the sexual scale couldn't be more cleverly investigated than in Thomas S. Roche's "Kinsey Six."

The score is even in this collection—if a girl's a slave in one story (as in C.D. Formetta's "Everything That You Want"), she's in command in another (Rachel Kramer Bussel's sizzling "His Just Rewards"). Foursomes give way to one-on-one action. Lovemaking behind closed doors (as in Lee Minxton's delicious "In Brendan's Room") is perfectly balanced by the unbelievably adventurous and outgoing couple in creative genius Tom Piccirilli's masterful tale "Dostoyevsky." There are one-night stands and long-term love affairs, women who do it for money, and girls who know for sure that money can't buy you love.

There's longing (in Gwen Masters' "Your Old Shirt") and fantasies come to life (in Sheri Gilmore's "Pure Sin") and cops and robbers ("Jane Bond—Stirred, Never Shaken" by the multi-talented Lynne Jamneck). But most importantly, there's plenty of old-fashioned teasing....

Which, of course, is just the way I like it.

And I hope you do, too.

Alison Tyler
July 2005

...AND LESLIE
by Ayre Riley

I've always gotten song lyrics wrong. Or, more honestly, I've always *massacred* song lyrics. Doesn't stop me from singing them at the top of my lungs, though. In the car or in the shower, you can find me belting out any number of misheard words from my favorite tunes.

I don't mumble. I don't really care. You know that Hawaiian song, "Tiny Bubbles"? I always thought it was, "Tiny Bubbles make me want more lovers," and I still think that's a better lyric than the real one— "make me warm all over." My version has a sexier ring to it, I think. And it's the truth. Tiny bubbles *do* make me want more lovers.

As you might imagine, Karaoke is always an enlightening experience for me. I stare at the words flowing across the TV screen, and I stop mid-verse to exclaim, shocked, "So *that's* what he's been singing!" for instance, I always thought that "Bennie and the Jets" went: "She's got electric boobs, her mom has two." Imagine my surprise to learn it was "She's got electric boots / a mohair suit."

"But what are electric boots?" I asked Josh.

"Don't know, but they sound less painful than electric *boobs*," he asserted.

In the Bush song, "Everything Zen," I believed in my heart of hearts that handsome Gavin Rossdale was singing, "There's no sex in Ohio / There's no sex in Rhode Island," rather than "There's no sex in your violence / There's no sex in your violence." Much better news for Ohio and Rhode Island, I'd have to say.

So when Josh heard me crooning while cleaning, I truly didn't know that I had the song wrong. I've always believed the lyrics were "Life could be ectacy, you and me and Leslie."

"Endlessly," he said, putting his strong arms around my slender waist and holding me close to his body. I felt the warmth of him, even through his clothes, and I stopped mid-dust and relaxed against him.

"You and me and Leslie endlessly?"

"There is no Leslie."

"*Of course*, there's a Leslie," I said, thinking about our svelte next-door neighbor with the gorgeous smile and the long, red hair.

"Not in the song."

I tried to figure out what he was saying. He let go of my waist and walked over to our old-fashioned hi-fi. While I watched, he backed up the record and we listened again.

"I swear," I said, "He's saying, 'Life could be ecstacy, you and me and Leslie.'"

Josh shook his head. "Endlessly. You and me *endlessly*."

"Well, let's ask her."

"What do you mean."

"You and me," I grinned. "And Leslie."

He stared for a minute, his gray-blue eyes open wide, then watched dumbstruck as I put down the pretty pink feather duster and reached for the cream-colored Princess phone on the side table.

"Why not just go over?" he asked.

"You're serious?"

"If you are."

So we went next door together and knocked. Leslie opened up immediately, almost as if she'd been expecting us. Had she heard the sound of the music from across the hall? Did she know the hidden meaning behind that oldie from the seventies? For a moment, we were all silent. She looked at Josh, then at me, and then she smiled. "You need a cup of sugar?"

"Something sweet," I assured her, grabbing hold of her hand and pulling her back across the hall to our place.

"Here," I said, pushing her gently into our over-stuffed blue velvet chair. "Listen and tell me what you think." I backed up the needle once more.

"Vinyl," she said, flabbergasted.

"That's not what I want you to hear."

The song played again and Leslie immediately smiled. "One of my all-time favorites."

"But what is he saying?"

"Life could be ecstasy—"

And now, before she could finish, I bent at her side on the floor, put my hand on her bare thigh and said, "You and me ...*and Leslie*?"

Her dark green eyes flashed. I saw flecks of gold swirling in their depths. "Yeah," she nodded. "I can see how someone might get that idea."

Josh made his way to the other side of the chair now, and he put his hand on Leslie's other leg. She was wearing little cut-off denim shorts, and I could already imagine pulling them off her and tossing them aside. Did she have a thong underneath? Or simple cotton panties? Or nothing at all?

"But could *you* get that idea?" he asked softly.

She answered by pulling her rose-pink tank top over her head, revealing her beautiful breasts which I had previously seen only shrouded by the tight tops she wore. Or by her green bikini when she was down swimming laps at the condo pool, her body glistening, her long hair shiny and wet. I leaned forward and started to touch her, and she tossed her thick hair back and shut her eyes. God, was she pretty. Waiting for us to pleasure her. Giving herself over to us. Josh worked with me, his hands caressing her sleek thighs, his fingers darting up to her button fly and starting to work it open. He pulled her cut-offs down her legs while I began to kiss and lick at her hardening nipples. When he reached for her panties, Leslie whispered, "Why don't we go to the bedroom?"

That made sense. There was no way that the three of us would fit into this recliner, no matter how comfortable or velvety. Leslie stood and led us down the hallway in our own apartment, and I shed my clothes on the way, nearly tripping over myself in order to get to her. I pulled off my white T-shirt and kicked out of my short summery skirt. When I reached the bedroom, she was already sprawled out in the middle of the mattress, her panties off, her body long and stunning, freckles dotting her pale skin like a magical constellation.

Josh hesitated at the doorway, watching as I instantly made myself at home between our neighbor's luscious thighs, as if I did this every day, and not just in my dreams. I kissed and licked my way right to her center, not spending too much time on foreplay, because I was too hungry for her. We could go slow another time, when I was consumed by a different song. Right now, the melody in my head contained one message only: *make her come*. And for once, I didn't have the lyrics wrong. I knew every word. Every single note. The dark red hair between Leslie's thighs was neatly trimmed, and I smiled as I realized she was a rare breed: a true redhead. I parted her kitty lips and started to lick between them, circling her clit with my tongue, then tapping on it to the music still playing in my mind.

Life could be ecstacy, repeated over and over—you and me *and* Leslie.

Oh, but where was the "you and me"? At the moment, there was only "me and Leslie," and that was fine for the start. I dove into her, lapping at her flood of juices, feeling that satiny wetness coating my face as I pressed firmly against her. I pictured how I like Josh to eat me, and I mimicked every move. *This* was ecstacy. This was what the man must have been singing about.

Josh waited as long as he could. He let me have her all to myself, my tongue piercing between her nether lips, my hands roaming over her soft, supple skin. Skin I'd admired for so many months, each time I saw her down in her emerald green bikini at the condo pool, each time I watched her in her short cut-offs and skimpy halter tops. But finally, he reached his limits. A man can only take so much stimulation.

Coming to the side of the bed, he maneuvered my body so that he had the access that he craved. Then, while I continued to trick my tongue against Leslie's sweet pussy, Josh gripped into my hips and slid his cock inside of me. He pumped me once, hard, and then held on tight, letting me grow accustomed to being sandwiched between two lovers. Then he started to move, slowly at first, and I groaned at the immediate pleasure that swam through me. The way his cock felt was almost too delicious. He was filling me up, taking me fiercely with a barely restrained power while I continued to tongue-fuck her. I could tell that Josh was in awe of the moving picture before him. Every time I sighed, he sighed. Every time Leslie moved her body, shimmying sexily in the center of the mattress, he fucked me even harder.

I glanced in the mirror over our dresser and saw that the three of us were joined in the most deliriously sexy way possible. We would have made one hot fucking record jacket.

Josh worked to the beat that was already in my head, thrusting hard and then pulling back, trailing his fingertips along my spine, caressing and tickling me as he fucked me. I employed the same methods to Leslie. My fingertips stroked her, my hair tickled her, my lips and tongue made magic over her clit.

Life could be ecstasy, I thought, feeling the pleasure rise up within me. *Can you feel it, too, Leslie?*

As Leslie came, she wrapped her hands in my sleek dark hair and held my face to her body. Shudders worked through her, powerful and vibrant, and then she relaxed, limp on the mattress. The look on her face was one of pure...you guessed it...ecstasy. Josh took this opportunity to speed up the motion of his hips, slamming into me again and again. I pressed myself against Leslie's leg, gaining contact with her smooth creamy skin, my clit making love to her calf, coming one second before Josh did. When he let loose inside of me, Leslie pulled me up her body and kissed me, and then the three of us snuggled against one another, bodies sticky, limbs overlapping.

We were silent for several minutes, and I could hear the needle skipping against the record in the other room. Rutting against the paper label over and over, in a futile attempt to make more music. But we had all the music we needed right here, in a bed filled with the quiet sounds of satisfied breathing.

And after a minute, I said, "Now, can anyone tell me what the fuck he's saying in Blinded by the Light?" and Leslie collapsed into giggles.

BETTER THAN SEX
by Dante Davidson

"What is?" the attractive brunette next to me at the bar asked.

"Excuse me?"

"Excuse *me*," she said with a smile that glimmered in her jade-colored eyes. "I couldn't help but overhear. And I heard you say *it* was better than sex. But I didn't hear *what* was. I don't mean to be rude, I'm just curious."

My best friend Liam smirked into his beer, obviously as interested in my response as the brunette. How the hell was I going to get myself out of this one? That's what his smirk said.

"Well, you know—" I told her, trying to sound sensitive as I stalled for time. "*Lots* of things." My mind raced. I didn't want to reveal what Liam and I had just been discussing, but I didn't want to tell her to mind her own business, either. Not a pretty thing like her.

"Name three," she said, a challenge in her voice. Liam smirked again. This time, with sound effects. I heard him chortling as he tried his best to look deeply interested in the little white cocktail napkin stuck to the bottom of his Pilsner.

"Three," I mused, as if it were difficult to whittle down the long list in my head to *only* three.

"Three," she repeated, as if she didn't think I could do it.

"Let's see," I said, trying to look as if I went around all the time listing things that were better than sex. "Well, gosh, there's walks on the beach, of course." I held up my thumb to indicate number one. "And holding hands, that's two." My pointer went up. "And...and... sunsets." No my middle finger joined the others.

She closed her hand over mine, shutting my fingers back down to zero, and nullifying my attempt. I liked the feel of her hand on mine, and I took in the fact that she wasn't wearing a wedding ring, and that her nails were a short, practical length, but painted a vibrant glossy red. "You sound like a Hallmark card." She looked as if she were going to be sick. Liam echoed her expression, and I nudged him with my elbow. I didn't care what *he* thought of my list. I wasn't trying to impress him, just her.

"All right," I said, with a nod, as if that first attempt had simply been a warmup, as if I hadn't been serious about those suggestions. As I gathered my thoughts, I noted with pleasure that she was drinking a black and tan. No frou-frou drink for her. "How about hot air balloon rides, champagne in bed, and cuddling by a fire?"

Now, she kicked me, her high-heeled fuchsia sandal connecting firmly with my shin. "Five points off for using the word 'cuddling.'"

"I didn't know we were keeping score."

"I always keep score," she said, matter-of-factly. "And I know what you're doing."

"At least one of us does," I grinned.

"You're telling me what you *think* women want to hear," she said, correctly assessing the situation. And I was. Or, more specifically, I was telling her exactly what my ex-girlfriend Sandy would have wanted to hear. But while Sandy might have been impressed by all six of my suggestions, they didn't seem to be working with this minx. I stammered, trying to defend myself, but she continued before I could come up with a decent explanation.

"I want to know what you told *him*," she nodded toward Liam, who was clearly staying out of this. "What you told him was better than sex."

Oh, Jesus. The thing was, we'd been talking about my ex. A girl who firmly believed in Hallmark card sentiments. She'd probably have exploded with bliss at the thought of holding hands *while* walking on the beach *at* sunset. The use of 'cuddling' would have won me points rather than lost them. She'd actually screamed at me during our break-up shouting match that shopping for shoes was better than sex, and *that's* what I'd just told Liam. (I didn't know if she'd meant sex in general or just sex with me. I was hoping for the former, but believed she meant the latter.) Most of our relationship had been based on fighting and making up. Fighting when she found a copy of *Penthouse* under a stack of more acceptable magazines. Making up when I brought her a bouquet of spring flowers in apology—not that I thought there was anything wrong with *Penthouse*, but I hated the sniffs and huffs and irritated glances she sent my way for the two days we weren't speaking. It had become something of a game for me, trying to win her back every time, trying to forcibly pry her from her uptight shell.

What I'd finally realized at the end was that the shell was empty. But it had been so long since I'd had good sex, and the brunette was so pretty, and I was a bit brainwashed after a year of being told that I wasn't sensitive enough, that I didn't know how to proceed. Luckily, the girl at my side had no such qualms.

"So," she continued. "Tell me, and we'll see if I agree with you."

I took a deep breath. Liam stared at the TV screen, but I could tell he wasn't watching the game. Not anymore.

"It wasn't what *I* thought," I explained. "It was what my ex-girlfriend thought."

"And—"

"Well," —*oh, Christ. What to say? Make something up or go for the truth?* — "She said that shoe shopping..."

The woman started to giggle. "You're kidding."

"You know, that's what I told her, and that's when she threw a shoe at me—"

"A Manolo?"

"Naw," I shook my head. "Nothing that sexy."

"Did she have a foot fetish?"

"Not that I'm aware of. I didn't find any sort of fetish at all with her—" I saw that Liam was shaking his head along with me. He hadn't approved of Sandy from the start when she'd made a fuss about poker night at our house. Any woman who disapproved of harmless card playing and testosterone-laden bullshit sessions didn't sit well with him.

"Course, *your* shoes are different," I said, indicating the one she'd kicked me with. "I mean, I could see how shopping for something like that—" the creation was truly delectable with tiny straps that wrapped around her delicate ankles and showcased her long, lean legs.

"Christian Laboutin," she smiled. "But I call them my 'sex in heels.'"

I don't know at what point she leaned in closer to me, or when the conversation changed from a titillating discussion to a flat-out come on, but right then, I started to feel a little warm.

"You know, shoe shopping could be sexy," she said, "if you were shopping with the right person."

"Well, *anything* could be—" I agreed. "I mean, even strolls on the beach *could* be sexy if you were with the right person."

"Or sunsets," she agreed.

"Or hot air balloon rides."

"Or holding hands—"

We were both smiling now.

"Or drinking champagne—" I said.

"Or walking a stranger out to her car—"

I nodded, "Yeah. That could be really sexy."

"So could fucking her up against the back of it," she said, her voice so low that only I could hear it.

"Oh, yeah," I said, sucking in my breath. "Yeah, I think that would be the top of my list."

I pulled out my wallet and set a bill down on the counter. The girl slid off her barstool and reached for her purse. She started walking ahead of me toward the entrance of the bar, but Liam put out a hand to stop her as she passed him. "You play cards?" he asked, as if he were the bouncer and this was the test to get into an exclusive club.

"What do you think?" she poker-faced him right back.

Liam smiled and let go of her wrist, then gave me the "she's all right" nod. But I didn't care what Liam thought. I was on my own for this one.

I followed her out of the bar to the parking lot behind. Even her car was sexy, a bright blue mint-conditioned Mustang. I couldn't fucking believe it. But then maybe it was my lucky night. Maybe someone up there liked me. Maybe I'd paid my dues for the past year, and this was my reward.

Maybe I should stop thinking and start doing.

At the car, the brunette turned to face me. There was a tie at the hip of her dress, and she pulled it loose. Suddenly, the cobalt silk dress she was wearing opened up, revealing a bra and panty set the exact same color as her shoes—a deep, almost violent shade of pink. I took a step closer to her, and she slid the dress off her body and tilted her head, looking at me, a challenge in her eyes. In moments, we were in a clinch. I had my hands in her shiny brown hair, my lips against her neck. Her skin was warm and soft, and when I kissed her, I smelled a scent like honeysuckle. I moved my lips down the front of her body, kissing her breasts through her satiny bra until I had to feel them naked under my hands. I popped the clasp on the bra and she helpfully shrugged off that tiny bit of fabric so that I had the access I craved. Her breasts were absolutely perfect, no bigger than a handful, and when I stroked my thumbs over her nipples, they responded instantly, growing harder under my touch. The woman moaned and arched her back, and I started to suckle from her breasts, first one, then the other, until I couldn't stand the suspense. I needed more.

Before I could act, though, she looked down at me.

"Take off your shirt," she said, her voice close to begging. I was quick to oblige, unbuttoning my worn denim oxford and tossing it onto the back of her car. Her fingers instantly stroked my naked skin, palming my shoulders, touching my chest, before pushing me down.

Slowly, I moved lower and lower until I had to bend my knees on the cement so that I could press my face to the very split between her legs. She leaned back against her car, and she sighed hard as I licked her through her panties.

"Take them off," she demanded.

I did so at once, slipping her knickers down her legs and waiting for her to step out of them. I liked the way she looked in just her heels. The thought of shoe shopping flickered in my head again. Yeah, shoe shopping could be sexy. If you knew you were going to get to do this at the end of the day.

I leaned forward again, now to taste her without any barrier. Sweetness flooded to greet my tongue. She was so wet. Had she gotten aroused talking to me at the bar? Had she been thinking about this the whole time? I didn't know, and I didn't really care. I only wanted to taste her, to flick my tongue against her clit while stroking my hands up and down her naked legs. She shuddered as I worked her, and I could feel the power of her pleasure under my fingertips. Then she gripped onto my thick dark hair and held me firmly against her, and I knew that she was going to come if I continued. I made slow circles around her clit, then sucked hard on it until she cried out. When she came, those magic shivers pulsed through her body, and the moan she let loose made me harder than I've ever been.

As soon as she composed herself, she turned around, offering me her body from behind. I stared at her creamy ass, and then ripped open the buttonfly of my jeans, releasing my ready hard-on.

"What's your name?" I asked as I slipped the head inside her. Warm wetness overpowered me. I had to grip onto the luscious curves of her hips to stay steady.

"Gemma," she sighed, her body trembling.

"I'm Nate," I said, shaking my head at the realization that I was introducing myself as my cock throbbed inside her.

"Pleased to meet you," she said, suddenly giggling as she must have realized the same thing. But her laughter was quick to subside as I brought one hand around to the front of her body and stroked her clit while I fucked her. I couldn't get enough of her body. I wanted to touch her all over at once, to learn each part of her, to memorize every line, every dip.

I slammed my body against hers as the pleasure built within me, and she stayed right with me, arching her hips to give me the best access, using her own hand on top of mine to show me how she wanted me to touch her. Fast and hard. Our fingers sliding together in her abundance of juices. I breathed in honeysuckle again and I wondered whether it was a perfume or if it was actually her own sexy scent.

When I could wait no longer, I hissed, "I'm going to—"

"Yes—" she said, as if agreeing. "Yes, yes, yes—"

As I came, I lifted her off the ground with the power of my thrusts, and then I felt her body respond as she came right after me, the spasms wracking her, the contractions milking me. We stayed locked together, drenched, her body nearly nude, mine half-dressed. When we parted, I reached for the silk dress, but she shook her head and picked up my old blue oxford shirt instead. She slid it on, and then opened the door to her car and climbed inside. I followed her, and we sat in the front seat, grinning at each other foolishly, both of us obviously pleased with ourselves.

"You know, I've seen you before," she admitted as I stared at the way she looked in only my shirt and high heels.

"Yeah?"

"I know you come out here with your friends on Fridays. I've been waiting for the right moment to break the ice. You gave me the perfect opener."

I couldn't help but smile. Who would have thought that bitching about my ex would have won me a ticket to paradise.

"But I really have to ask you something," and now Gemma grinned back at me.

"Anything."

"What's better than sex?"

"We're not going there again, are we?"

"I mean, to you. I want to know what you really think. Not what you think some girl wants to hear."

"Nothing," I told her, pulling her close as I felt myself get ready for another round. "Not a fucking thing."

CALL ME JENNY
by Savannah Stephens Smith

The denim was soft, but underneath was steely. Hard. The erection only achieved by men still under twenty-five. To me, they're boys, not men, but the way he wanted me wasn't boyish. Not in the least.

We sat in my driveway in the suburbs after a long winter journey. Brent was my son's friend, and he'd given me a ride home. It had started at the international airport in the city. The last flight of my trip home was canceled due to bad weather, and Brent was at the airport, too, dropping off his roommate before heading back to his—and my—hometown. Brent's friend's flight had left, but mine hadn't. It was funny, running in him at Domestic Departures, a familiar face in a crowd of disgruntled strangers who all wanted to get to home and holidays. Instead of leaving me to wait for the next flight, Brent offered to take me with him. The snowy weather didn't deter him from a seven-hour drive—that's the way the young are.

Something made me accept his invitation—maybe I didn't want to face a night alone in a hotel in the city where my ex-husband and his new and much younger wife lived. Maybe I just wanted to get home, the sooner the better. At any rate, I said "yes." Brent fetched my luggage and we left the airport together. The last leg of my journey home would be with my son's childhood best friend. Odd, but it was better than travelling alone, and we'd known each other for years. It would be a nice chance to catch up on what he'd been doing since he graduated from university in spring.

We'd driven through the winter day, afternoon quickly becoming evening as we left the city behind and began to weave through the mountains. Due to the winter conditions, we travelled more slowly than if it had been summertime. I was glad Brent handled his car with caution, and I wondered if my son would be so mature. Somehow, I doubted it.

As we moved onward through the night, Brent updated me on recent events in his life. He'd started a job as an accountant with a large firm in the city, and he'd broken up with his girlfriend. He had moved into an apartment downtown with another friend from university and was enjoying the big city. Of course he was: Brent was young, good-looking, with a bright future. Single, too. He didn't need to ask about Robbie—we both knew my son's prospects were less promising. Robbie had dropped out of school the prior year and was now attempting to beat the very long odds in the music biz. Working at minimum-wage jobs behind the counter at a CD store and behind the bar at clubs supplemented his income. If other things also supplemented his income, I didn't want to know. I could only hope his father would be able to keep Robbie in line, but I doubted it.

Being in a car together lent the two of us an unexpected intimacy. As if under the spell of the snow falling in the headlights, the black and white night, and the cautious speed of travel, our talk turned quite frank a few hours into the journey. We discussed life and learning, love and sex. I couldn't believe the boy I'd seen grow up was now a man, but he was. Dark haired, muscular, with nice, even features. From what I could tell, he hadn't picked up the trend of tattooing and piercing whatever body part happened to be sticking out at any given time—unlike my son. As the trip progressed, the feeling of intimacy intensified. We were relaxed with each other now, and I felt as if we were friends, not an older woman and a young man who she thought of as being much like a son. I suppose I flirted with Brent more than I should have, surprised to find myself enjoying his discomfort—and his arousal. I suspected he'd become erect when we'd talked about sex, because he shifted uncomfortably in the driver's seat. More than once I saw his hand automatically go down to adjust himself before he halted the gesture. I teased him, enjoying his blushes and brushes with confession. By the time we arrived at the lights of town, I'd let the situation go too far, though, and I figured he was stiff as a plank. And by the time we reached my neighborhood he wasn't the only one itching for a little sheet-slipping.

By then I was wet and acutely aware of how sometimes life could be very drab without a husband—without a man, anyway. I'd been squeezing my thighs together for the past hour, aching for relief. Home. A bottle of wine, the hot tub, and my vibrator. Suddenly what had seemed so delightful when I was stuck at the airport on the coast now seemed dismal. The glamorous life of a single woman over forty. Hell, at this rate, I wouldn't even need the vibrator. A glass of wine and the hot tub jets would probably give me an orgasm. An orgasm for one. It seemed so bleak.

When Brent turned the ignition off in my driveway, I leaned over and touched him, and he froze. Shock, embarrassment—enjoyment? But he didn't push my hand away, and he didn't protest. I stroked his hard-on through his jeans, fascinated, as he squirmed beneath my touch. Clearly, he'd gotten quite aroused by our talk. I bet he'd come in his jeans if I kept it up. I didn't want that. Not while I needed it more than his Levi's did.

"Come into the house, Brent," I murmured. "You need something to keep you up." He still had a way to go, now that his parents no longer lived three doors down from me. "A cup of coffee. Or..." Me, of course.

It wasn't nice to tease him, but the agony in his eyes was matched by desire. I knew that I looked good, and that this young man wanted me. And it wasn't all teasing—I needed some relief, too. Winter's cold. I was hot. And life's short.

We slogged inside, shaking snow from our shoes and shivering at the chill of an empty house. In the kitchen, I stopped pretending. Maybe it was looking around at the same old "dream kitchen" where I'd spent far too much time, the dream worn thin long ago, or maybe it was knowing my husband was never coming back, but I dropped the notion that I was going to make Brent some coffee before he continued on his journey. I had a much better way to thank him.

Impulsively, I dropped to my knees in front of him, probably frightening him. But he'd followed me into the house, hadn't he? He was a gorgeous thing. And his parents had raised him well— even with an impressive erection, the outlines of which I could clearly see—he struggled to remain polite.

"Mrs. Douglas?" he whispered, but I had difficulty believing he was that nervous. He was twenty-two, for heaven's sake. They're nurtured on R-rated movies, must-see-TV, and trash-talking music these days, and I knew he'd had girlfriends all through high school and university. He and Robbie had been friends for years.

"Yes, Brent," I cooed, drawn to that tantalizing bulge. I couldn't remember the last time I'd seen an erection that hard in real life, and I couldn't help but stroke him more. My daring made my stomach flutter and my pussy quiver. A warm wanting sensation urged me on. His thighs were just fine, too. And did I mention his ass? Oh, my. Soccer? Running? What sport had sculpted him? It should be mandatory for all males to partake of whatever made him so...healthy.

"What are you doing, Mrs. Douglas?"

"Call me Jenny. Honey, that thing looks like it's going to rip right through those jeans," I purred, fully aware I was acting out every cliché I'd come across from mainstream romance to triple-X-rated videos. How often do you get a chance to do it in real life? I had the chance to live out one of those afternoon fantasies, and I was going to take it. After all, it wouldn't be as if he were unwilling. His erection said "ready, willing, and very much able."

"I bet you don't want to show up at your house sporting this," I said, rubbing his hard-on. The genie was going to be out of the jeans soon. I desperately wanted it inside me. The ache intensified.

"No ma'am. My mother would..."

"Yep."

A rueful chuckle from us both, because we both knew what his mother was like. Prissy, perfect Patricia... I never liked her, and she felt the same way, despite our sons' friendship. I didn't want to think about that, though. I was a mother, but I was also a woman.

With that, I put any maternal comparisons aside and surrendered to anticipating being a woman in a man's arms.

"I bet if I were you—" I started, itching to undo the copper snap of his jeans and tug the zipper down. Brent looked like he was blessed with about seven—maybe even a smidge more—inches. Thick, too. I couldn't believe I was licking my lips, but I did. I wanted him, the urge sharp, strong and beyond denying. "—I'd probably pull over as soon as you were out of sight of my house, and I'd have that thing out...is it as big as it looks? Never mind. I'll...." Find out, I thought, but didn't say it. I didn't want to scare him. "And finish myself off in, what? One, two, three strokes, tops?"

Brent was breathing pretty hard by then, standing there in front of me, but he hadn't bolted. Not yet. The nice hard-on was beginning to look a little painful, in fact, and I could make out the shape and get a good idea of the generous size of the thing. I guess the way I kept touching him as I talked wasn't helping matters much, either. "Mrs. Douglas," he muttered.

"Honey, why don't we take care of that thing in a much better way?" I squeezed, and he groaned. "Do an old lady a favor."

"You're not old," he protested, still polite.

I got up. "You're very kind."

"You're very pretty," he added, shy as a suitor.

"I'm very horny, Brent," I said, and kissed him. Hard. It was the wrong thing to do. But he was kissing me back in under a second with no time to change our minds. Then his tongue was thrusting in my mouth, hot and eager, if a little unskilled. I liked it. We kissed, surrendering to impulse.

In a minute, I pulled back. I couldn't believe I was trying to seduce him. But my body craved, and I wanted him so badly. I was already breathing heavily and aching to rip off my sweater. I was wet. And so very bad. Life is so short, though.

If I thought about it for more than a second, I'd... This time, Brent kissed me, eyes closing, yielding to want. I forgot who he was and only felt how he was: hard and eager, solid and strong, young and healthy. He pulled me close and I swayed against his crotch, rubbing myself against that tantalizing bulge. I'd felt plumber's pipes with more give than that. I wanted it. He backed me into the tiled countertop and ground his pelvis against mine, sucking my tongue desperately. What he lacked in technique, he made up for in intensity and enthusiasm. I didn't mind—it excited me all the more. We stopped kissing only long enough for me to pull my sweater over my head and fling it to the floor. I was wearing a plain white tee beneath it, and my favorite jeans. They were three sizes smaller than I'd worn as Stanley's wife. I was my own woman now. I could do what—or who—I wanted. All woman, all curves and desire.

I tilted my head and sought Brent's mouth again. Both of us were hungry, appetites raging in the silence of the house where he'd visited as a boy. Now, he'd entered the house as a man. I found his hands and brought them to my breasts, and he groaned and squeezed. My nipples poked against the cotton, and I couldn't wait for him to touch them. They were aware and sensitive. I wanted touch: hand or mouth, I didn't care which. Oh, mouth, I thought, teasing his tongue with mine. Brent smelled great. He was taller than I. He probably outweighed me by fifty pounds. When had that happened? I felt dizzy.

He wore a navy polo shirt under his jacket, and I tugged it out of his jeans as we kissed, frantic to touch his skin. His back was smooth and warm beneath my fingers, broad and strong. I thumbed the belt loop of his jeans, pulled him to me, and cupped his ass. I heard myself moan. I was damp; I could feel it against my panties. I hugged him harder, my legs spread, working against his erection, already making the motions of intercourse. Denim to denim. Want to want. Age was meaningless. Blood and desire overrode everything.

I pulled his shirt out, sliding my hand up his belly, flat and hard, and found his chest. Warm and muscular, he was beautifully made. Beautifully male. I longed to nip at his skin, to flick his nipples, kiss my way down...

We stopped kissing long enough for him to yank his jacket off. It joined my sweater on the floor. I pulled my tee up and his hands were on my breasts, with only the bra between his hand and my skin. I hissed with pleasure as he seized me. My nipples were throbbing hard bits that demanded touch. I wanted to rip my bra off. Instead, we kissed some more. It looked like Brent wasn't in any hurry to get to his folks' house now.

I pulled the tee all the way off, wriggled out of the bra and set my breasts free. Brent groaned, and his hands sought them, caressing my bare skin. He nuzzled me, moving from one to the other, in a fever to taste and touch. I touched him, too, revelling in being explored. His hair was soft, but his mouth was driving me crazy. When he finally took one firm nipple between his lips, I made a sound like a cat. He paused, but my groan of pleasure told him to continue. He sucked my nipples as I stroked his hair and his shoulders. His mouth was hungry on my breasts, and the more he sucked, the wetter I got. His mouth and hands sent hot pangs of desire all through me, ending in my clit and deep inside my pussy.

Hours of being pleasantly horny had culminated in desire that would not be satisfied by anything less than fucking. Hard fucking. Brent's mouth was like fire on my nipples, exactly what I'd been craving as we drove, appetite building with each mile. I had been covertly touching myself as we travelled through the snowy night and talked dangerously about subjects that decorum said we should avoid. I had been confident the darkness hid my actions. Now, what I'd imagined was happening and it was bliss, sending me into deeper yearning.

At last, impatience drove me. I needed more, needed to feel his naked body, his skin along mine. I wanted to undress him, discover him, to finally see what he looked like. Brent sucked one proud nipple, his tongue rasping over the tip and making me writhe with longing. I wriggled my jeans down my hips, aching, wondering for a millisecond if he could smell it on me. Probably. I didn't care. I'm a bitch in heat, I thought, and palmed his pecs like he did my tits. Brent lifted his head from my skin, and we kissed. His mouth was warm, his lips soft, but his tongue was wonderfully lewd. Would he touch me? My pussy? I wriggled and squirmed, pressing my breasts against his shirt, standing there with my jeans pulled down. Never had I felt so wicked.

Brent groped between my opened legs and I moved against his hand, clutching his shoulders. Palm and fingers moved against me. I groaned when his finger sunk into my wetness. He stroked me, finding my nipple again, and I swayed against his fingers. I could almost, but not quite, climax from the touch of his stillnovice, half hesitant hand alone. But it wouldn't feel as good as it would to come, tight around his cock, climaxing with that singular feeling of being filled.

I slid against one crooked finger, dancing on the edge of orgasm, and then drew back. Fuck me, I thought, but didn't say it, certain the spell would be broken if I voiced what we were doing. It all seemed like a dream, a housewife's three-in-theafternoon fantasy. Soap stars and neighborhood boys fuelling desire men like my husband left burning, unquenched. I stood, breathing hard, stroking his taut belly, then moved my hand down to palm his cock. I pressed hard, and he made a sound.

"You must be uncomfortable," I said, and I finally got to work that brass button open. Unzipping him was a challenge, given how stiff he was, but I managed. Want finds a way. Sliding the zipper down over the length of his erection and hearing his rough breathing only excited me more. The zipper slowly went up and over the rigid bulge of his cock as I slid it open. Then his underwear was the only thing between what I wanted and me. I worked his prick out, crossing some boundary. It was an action I could never undo.

His cock was beautiful. It was all I'd idly dreamed of as we drove, simmering with longing: erect, warm and throbbing, nicely hefty. Brent groaned as I squeezed him, entranced by my prize and the shock of seeing his prick, real and urgent. No fantasy. Mine. Then I was on my knees before him in the clear light of the kitchen, kneeling on the oak floor. I clasped him, squeezed again, anticipating. I hadn't had anything that looked this appetizing in my kitchen for a very long time. Brent's cock was nicely shaped, thick enough to make my brows fly upward, and a healthy shade of pink. He was circumcised. Even as I knew I was being one very naughty lady, I loved the way I felt in the midst of this. Brazen, bold, and bad. My jeans pulled down, my breasts bared and nipples swollen. I was completely lost to lust, high on sinning. "I'm so wet," I confessed—or bragged—stroking the silky length of him, a clear drop collecting at the swollen tip. He was helpless to it. His prick was such a pretty thing, too, and I couldn't wait to—

I leaned in and slipped the swollen, velvety head of him between my lips. A shudder went though me as my tongue met his skin. Brent cried out a half-hearted protest. He was tender and warm and I circled the engorged crown of his penis with my tongue, teasing him. It was good. Careful, careful—he could go off any minute. I had a sudden urge to do it, to bring him off. To suck hard and feel him throb in my mouth, then lewdly swallow all he gave. But the itch between my legs wanted more. I needed to be fucked.

But first... I sucked him, my throat filled with a man for the first time in what felt like years. I gloried in it, my breasts bared and my panties pulled down, pussy wet and pouting for the cock I tongued. I licked and sucked him until Brent's fingers tightened in my hair and he sounded as if he were about to erupt. "Ah!" he cried out above me, his prick thick in my throat, my right thumb gentle on his warm, heavy balls. They had drawn up, tightening as I sucked. His cock was getting bigger, swelling. He was close. I swayed on my knees, half-stripped, a lewd vision. My left hand cupped one heavy breast before tangling in my pubic hair, then returning to my tits. Brent wasn't the only one close to orgasm. His cock was yearning in my mouth as my tongue slid along the underside, making him quiver. It was perfect debauchery. I slid one finger inside me, slippery when wet, oh yes. I was ready. I squeezed him with my right hand, sucked hard, and slowly eased my mouth down his cock until I only had the glans captured. I licked it one last time. "Fuck me," I demanded. I sank down, resting on my thighs, my legs spread open. The invitation was clear. Hell, I probably dripped it on the floor.

Brent was down there with me, kissing me, his hands warm on my bare ass. I rose to meet him. His cock poked my belly, and then nudged lower. I twisted up to find it, but was constricted by my jeans. I collapsed, saw the ceiling in a blur, and then he was over me, yanking my jeans down, frantic, his knee working to open my legs. Denim trapped. He kissed me again, his tongue thrusting hot and hard like I wanted his penis to. We wrestled a bit, getting closer and closer, and I felt the blunt head of his cock nudging me, but it was only a tease. His knees weren't up to the oak floor that I loved, and neither was my ass. The surface was cool and unforgiving, and we weren't getting anywhere.

"Over there," I gasped, wriggling in the direction of the foyer, where the kitchen became a wide hall and the carpeting began.

I crawled on my hands and knees, and I didn't have time to feel stupid, for Brent was scrabbling with me, then reaching for my breasts. I knelt, and from behind me, he cupped them, gently twisting my nipples. Underneath the imperious ticking of my grandfather clock, he got my jeans off, and I bucked against his hand as it explored me once more. Fingers in my curls, then fingers in my hot, slippery folds. I turned to face him, clutching him, swimming in fire. Then I reached down and clasped him. He was beautiful, the right thing to hold. He fit my hand like a tool crafted just for me. I marvelled at how warm his skin was, silky and hard.

I pulled Brent's jeans down, and he got loose. We didn't say a word. I went down on my back, and the carpeting was a better surface for our urgent pairing. Cupping his luscious little ass, tight and firm, I kissed him as his cock prodded my thigh. He still wore his shirt, his belly flat and hard beneath the hem, his cock rearing up dangerously below. I was underneath him, opening my legs without restraint now, and then Brent was over me in the ancient position. So close.

He shifted, kneeling over me. Don't change your mind now! I lifted my hips, found his prick, rubbed against it. His face tightened. I couldn't tell if it was desire or torment. "God—I haven't done..." he gasped.

"Don't tell me you're a virgin," I said, as his hands cupped both my breasts. He *couldn't* be a virgin. His mouth traced the slope of my breast as I trapped the head of his penis and began to work it into me. It was driving me crazy—I was so close to what I wanted. Needed. Brent didn't kiss, or move, like a virgin. Just like a young man who'd been without it for far too long. He sought my nipple, risen high and dark pink with excitement, urgently. He sucked for a long moment, before he spoke, voice husky. "No, ma'am. I just haven't—I mean, not much. Too busy..."

Too busy? Good grief, he had more discipline than I'd ever

had when I was twenty-two. But then, hadn't his ex-girlfriend been much like him? Quiet, religious, a good student? Everything my son wasn't, kids I hoped would be good influences. And here I was, seducing Brent. Some mother I was. I was about to... I didn't want to think. I wanted to fuck. "Please!" I cried, and he shoved hard and entered me. Despite the wetness, I was newly tight. It had been so long I'd forgotten what it really felt like to open my legs and let a man inside me, to trust it would give me pleasure.

It was both familiar and strange to feel it about to begin. I drew my knees up and changed the angle, and then he was sliding all the way into me with slow, exquisite friction. It almost hurt, but it felt so good.

Tentative at first, then his strokes quickened, his face a stranger's. He seized my arms and pumped savagely. He kissed me, his mouth impatient, then broke off. I met each thrust, close to climax. Each stroke got me a rung higher up the ladder. The ladder stretched to the sky, to infinity, and I wanted to go all the way up. "Fuck me," I begged him, clutching his shoulders, twisting the fabric of his shirt. I was soaring and sinning, and he was the only thing that kept me from flying into a million pieces.

Brent pounded into me, making me gasp, and if I was getting rug burns on my ass, I didn't care. No give of mattress made the penetration seem even more powerful, or maybe it was just his youth and my desperation. I wrapped my legs around his slim hips, and lifted my pelvis to meet his thrusts. I was there, tantalizingly close, on the verge of orgasm. This was the moment to hold. If I could have stayed like that forever, I'd offer my mortal soul with no regrets. And then I was coming, hard, rolling into the fire. Release made me cry out, the cold house no longer empty, full of my pleasure.

Too soon it was over, the tide rolling out, Brent still fucking me. I lay there, beneath him, gasping, heart beating a drumbeat to his thrusts. He made a noise to rival mine as he came, going stiff, trapped between my thighs, the sweetest prison a man can find. I watched him come, enjoying the pleasure twisting his face, and saw the man he was, not the boy he'd been. The man in that most private of moments. His climax was like him: strong, intense, somehow pure. Then it was over. He slowed, stopped, throbbing inside me.

"Oh, god," I said, as he panted above me, the only sound our breathing, the only result of pleasure my horror and the beat of my heart, unaccustomed to what we'd done. What we'd done... What had I done? Was it worth it?

His eyes were closed, and he looked... Happy. Drained. Blissful. Like I felt.

So, hell, yeah—it was worth it. Like Scarlet, I'd let tomorrow take care of itself. Life is short. Winter's cold. Pleasure is rare enough.

DOSTOYEVSKY
by Tom Piccirilli

I'm polite. When she asks me to hold the elevator, I thrust out my arm and block open the door. The fact that she's naked doesn't have a lot to do with it until after she's already gotten on. The zucchini and ping pong paddles are another matter altogether.

"Could you hit thirty-seven please?" she asks.

It's already lit. It's my floor. The same old question begins circling around my skull—am I heading for some good harmless fun here or diving straight into hell? In the six months since I'd left home I was running about 50-50.

I do what you're supposed to do in an elevator. I look straight ahead, but I've got damn good peripheral vision. We take it floor after floor and I'm trying to think of anything I can to keep my erection down. The new script of *Zypho: Critter from Beyond the Edge of Space*, how much I miss my mother's pasta fasulli, where the hell hotel security might be, and the fact that the Yankees are down 3-2 in the series. Why I'm working so hard doesn't make much sense, but you've got to hold on to your self-control for at least ten or twenty seconds. It's only right.

The naked woman holding two zucchinis and the red and green paddles turns to me and says, "Boy, you've got good control of your curiosity!"

"Listen," I tell her. "I'm a New York writer working in Hollywood. I'm trying to learn how to take everything I see for granted."

It doesn't appease her. "Well, don't miss out on a few new experiences along the way. Aren't writers supposed to be observant and adventurous?"

They are. I am. I've already noted how gorgeous she is, and my back teeth are grinding together so hard I can almost feel my fillings buckle. Christ, this town was built to drive me crazy. I tilt my jaw at her and let my gaze glide over her skin, and I'm barely able to hold back the animal groan from breaking inside my chest.

She has meat and curves in all the right places, and the motion of the elevator has given her body a consistent jiggle that's causing my pulse to break seventy, eighty, ninety.

Twenty-four years old or thereabouts, with a splash of red highlights in her brown hair that coils and loops to frame her face. One curl takes purchase at the edge of her mouth. It's a movie moment. I'm supposed to reach over, pull it free, ease my lips to hers. I'm Gary Cooper caught in *Cafe Flesh 3*.

She has a nice solid plumpness and genuine weight to her, and she's got enough conviction not to be made self-conscious by the starved will-o'-the-wisp image that L.A. promotes. Her tits are large with just enough sag that they wobble as the car progresses. The large aureole are pink, her desert rose nipples huge and pointed and somehow taunting.

We all have our thing. Mine is big tits with taunting desert rose nipples. The sweat writhes through my scalp and she smiles up at me beatifically. Her white teeth aren't capped, and her dark eyes are suddenly twinkling. Or maybe I'm just hyperventilate.

It's quite possibly the slowest elevator on the face of the earth. I'm polite but impatient, even when I'm enjoying the view.

"What kind of movies?" she asks.

The honest answer is low-budget horror flicks starring aging porno actresses trying to build up the "straight dramatic" roles on their resumes. I had started off with a script for Dostoyevsky's *Notes from Underground* and somehow ended up on the far side of the sun with Zypho, the brain-juice-drinking alien. If I thought about it for too long I wound up getting a migraine, so I tended to let it ride. "Independent erotic thrillers."

"Oh."

She says it like she sees through my smoke-screen but she gives a grin to show there's nothing to be ashamed of. We take our conceits where we can grab them. The smirk is dubious and full of fuck-me mystery.

"Okay," I tell her, "I give. Fill me in. Or should I just string it together and figure that you're a professional table tennis player who got hungry...but the kitchen was closed"—it's nearly three in the morning— "and you could only find a couple of spare zucchini left over on the lunch special buffet table...and...ah, you fell into the pool? Had to leave your clothes at the dry cleaners?"

"Pretty good story. Covered a lot of ground."

It's not Dostoyevsky but it'll do. "So then?"

"I'm working my way through graduate school as a model and performer for Dee Ess Magazine. They're holding their first convention here this weekend."

"Dee Ess?"

"*D/s Magazine*. Dominant-submissive lifestyle publications."

"Oh." It's the performer bit that's got me.

"There's about two hundred folks who showed."

"You're gonna need more vegetables to feed them all."

I worked my way through college selling magazine subscriptions. I have the overwhelming sense that she's making more money than I did.

"You're witty. But you're scared of me, aren't you?"

"No. I think you've been surrounded by too many subs lately."

"Why are you in the hotel? Did you come for the show? Are you here to watch people like me?"

My agent Monty Stobbs had gotten me this hotel room because I only had four days left to finish the script. Normally that wouldn't have been much of a problem, but at around midnight tonight the cops had raided the house next door to mine in East Hollywood and two wild shots had come through my bedroom window. Monty wanted me to weave my near-death experience into the movie. He thought that the brush with my own mortality would somehow work wonders on a sequel. *Zypho: the Post-modern Neo-expressionistic Morality Play*. It would lend more credence to the brain-juice-sucking scenes.

"My house is being renovated," I say.

When we hit the thirty-sixth floor she leans on the EMERGENCY STOP button and the elevator slams to a halt. I'm tossed sideways into her and suddenly my hard-on is jabbing her in the thigh and I've got a zucchini shoved into my armpit.

The perfect outline of muscles in her legs and belly are haunting, and the aggressive angle of her throat aims at me, as if she's arching it towards my teeth to chew. The west coast breeds a whole new kind of hang-up, but guilt about touching your pee-pee sure isn't one of them.

I say the first thing that clatters up into my head, which is never a good idea. "I don't like zucchini."

"I didn't intend to make you eat it."

"Well, okay then."

"Here." She hands me the red ping pong paddle. "Hit me. Spank me."

We all have our thing.

My repressions start slicing through me again, as I stand there thinking of Sunday afternoons in the basement playing doubles with my parents and sister. I give a tentative swat and the meat on her ass hardly moves.

"Harder!"

I squeeze my eyes shut and let loose with another smack. She squeals and I try not to picture my little sister in pig-tails scoring a point off my old man.

"This isn't working."

"Shit!"

Now comes the tinge of regret in her eyes, some of the disappointment leaking through. It relates a great deal. That expression speaks of sex and love, shame and audacity, brazenness, money, and courage. All of it is real, and I move in.

I sling the paddle into the corner behind my luggage, tear the other one out of her hand and give her one more swat on the ass. She yelps and stares at me with a new delight. You take control by force of will, not by volleying. I grab the goddamn zucchini and toss them aside too as I shrug out of my jacket and shirt.

"No no, I need that!"

"You don't need a fuckin' zucchini!"

I ease forward again, directing her to undo my fly. I don't know whether she's a submissive or a dominatrix, whether I'm playing into her kink or going against type, and I don't much give a shit. I want her.

She knows it, too, and that's when the game begins. She backs off, smiling, pressing her tits together like she's trying to wrangle a dollar from me. I step closer wondering when the fire department will come swinging down through the roof.

The power struggle flows back and forth between us.

She twists around and bends way over, as if I'm not worth looking at anymore. She rests her arms atop the little metal railing, showing off her ass, giving me the dance floor wriggle. It happens like this on occasion, I know, when you fall into a b-movie setting, trying to assert yourself upon a willing partner you've only met three hundred and sixty feet ago at ground level.

You've got to give in order to get. I run my hand around her, touching her neck softly, squeezing and showing her that I might be an emotional train wreck but I've still got some muscle. She moans because she understands as I trail my fingers down across her chest, her belly, slowly plying through the thatch of pubic hair to toy with her clit. I pluck it, tease it out. She hisses through her teeth and I let go.

"Don't stop."

"Turn around and unzip me."

"Do it yourself."

I pluck at her clit again and slip two fingers into her, hooking and pulling. This is tenuous ground, feeling one another out. You're always this close to getting slapped, going to jail, falling in love.

I want to tell her my name so I can hear her spit it out, but it's not that kind of situation. She murmurs and there's a husky snarl in her voice now, a thick whisper meant to drive me out of my head if I wasn't already gone. I've got her by the cunt and slowly turn her to face me.

"Unzip me."

"Oh yes," she says, not because she wants to give me pleasure but because we've moved on to the next round, when you've got to get your goodies out.

The beast in me starts taking over and the same old rage stirs and crawls up my back to settle in between my shoulders. She can see it, maybe it's an old story. Am I no different than the pale, pudgy studio heads who visit a convention like this to get their asses beat with a cat-o'-nine-tails? I can feel myself skidding into cliché as I lunge forward, reaching for her tits, and stop in mid-motion. I growl, angry at the set-up, thinking about how this will all look on the page. Where the cameras should go, what the shot list schedule will be.

She undoes my fly and pulls my pants down. I kick them backwards against my luggage. My hard-on tents my jockeys and she pinches her chin, inspecting, making me wait, staring at me from one angle, then another. My chest crawls with sweat and it drips down my stomach into my waistband. She scowls at me because I'm taking too long. I don't know what the next move is.

Maybe she expects me to tear my shorts off and ram into her mouth. Maybe I'm supposed to gurgle like a baby and ask her to powder my crotch and diaper my ass. How should I write an article addressed to the editors of D/s Magazine?

Zypho would already have his tentacles of love jammed into her ears sucking out all the naughty thoughts.

Zucchini has no smell but somehow I'm back at home for Sunday dinner and grandma is putting out a plate of fried slices and I'm having a very difficult time of staying focused. I can just imagine the fire chief with his red hat and ax chopping through the outer doors any minute. The second hand of my watch is snapping the moments off and I know I'm losing the rhythm, I've got about two more ticks before she takes her ping pong paddles and goes home.

I'm so hard I'm hitting that nice plateau of pain. This is where she wants me to be, what I'm supposed to be experiencing. The heat and the sudden anger is clouding my vision but I can hold on. You fight the battles worth fighting. I take her by the chin and instead of forcing her mouth open I gently lift her to her feet, take her in my arms, and press her into the corner. I arch her higher and higher until she catches on and helps me out. I lift her onto the rail and she eases her legs out, slides her feet along the walls and I bend to taste her.

"Oh," she says, almost giddy. "You're a good little boy."

"Talk your shit while you can," I tell her. "In a minute you'll be nothing but whimpers."

It's a pretty good line, and I think I should file it away, but then the page and the cameras finally recede and my face is inside her cunt. You can come back to the world this way.

I lap and lick and suck and take my time, and I'm not so polite anymore. Her outer lips are swollen pink and pliable as I kiss them the way I should be kissing her mouth. Passionate French kissing as it ought to be done. It lasts for a while. Then, with only the tip of my tongue, I move top to bottom, feeling her swell and constrict.

I take the edge of one inner lip and gnaw for a bit, switching back and forth. She immediately shudders and pushes her cunt out further, and I tongue her even harder. She trembles to a powerful tune as I flick my tongue, in control, watching all the right parts jiggling. My cock throbs viciously and I start humping air. I spread her further, holding my breath and going in deeper. Black spots dance in my eyes.

This is the kind of ridiculous shit that works its way into American myth. The fire chief hacking his way inside, finding me blue, unresponsive. Man drowns in freak elevator pussy fluid accident. The late night talk show hosts will bat it around for months.

She mewls and comes twice in quick succession as I continue to lick and suck, breathing her in, wiping my lips off on her thighs. She tries to talk, perhaps wanting to hurl an insult or indignity, but she whispers, then finally whimpers. The stupidest validation can make you feel like a man. This is your job to begin with.

She whines, "Enough…"

Thank Christ. I ease her down and she drifts forward into my arms and we hit the floor together, me on top. I still have my underwear on and she knows now what the next step has to be as she pulls them off me, swallows my cock, spits on it, works her hand over me, and then ushers me in between her legs. Sometimes there's foreplay and sometimes you've already had enough.

"Oy!" she says, and I champ my teeth against the flesh of her shoulder, hard enough to make her grimace but without breaking skin. She lets out a low moan checked by anguished snorts and says, "You can leave marks if you want. It's okay. Some guys like to see that."

It's almost enough to snap me loose, but I fight past the new thoughts, the faces of slobbering men in latex perusing bruises and bites. I grab under her knees and press her legs back, shoving in. She holds herself open as I work both my thumbs across her pussy lips. I drop on top again, sucking her nipple into my mouth, chewing, nibbling at the hard bud inside.

Maybe this is the only real way to face your own mortality. I might not be alive for any particular purpose, but if I am, this is as good a reason as any. It makes me laugh and I chuckle in her ear. It startles her for a second and then she joins in.

I thrust wildly into her and feel her rising up to meet me as she tightens around my shaft, so wet I feel her splashing against my groin. The veins in her throat thicken and every tendon and muscle stands out as she tenses and grunts her orgasm.

She doesn't slow down though, quickening her pace as she stares into my eyes and tries to capture something—my soul, my guilt—and reaches up to run her hands through my hair, obligingly, with some modicum of care.

It's all I need, that bit of love, as her tits bounce in time with my thrusting. My fists clench on the ripped loose threads of the elevator carpet and I hold on tightly, jammed against her and stiffening as I erupt. As I fill her, hearing the shattering glass of my bedroom window again, her pussy squeezes and releases.

I lay there on top of her panting while she giggles in my ear.

Now there will be a new set of wonders.

Do we sleep together tonight? Will we have breakfast across from one another in the morning, share the day, exchange names and numbers? Should we kiss? Is it wrong for me to ask her to lick my cock clean?

She hops up without a word and starts the elevator again. It bucks and rumbles as if echoing an orgasm. This must be part of the high, the possibility of getting caught with come sliding down your legs as the doors open and a mom and pop family stare in awe or disgust, hiding the eyes of the kids. I'm too tired to care much.

But no one is there when the bell rings.

I gather my clothes and luggage and she picks up her zucchini and paddles and we tramp down the hall. I don't feel liberated being naked and walking around like I own the place. I feel utterly silly.

I follow her in silence and find that our rooms are next to one another. Her door's been left propped open an inch. I hadn't even thought about where she might have a card key hidden.

She steps inside and the door closes with a gentle but resounding click. I go in and throw my stuff down, flop on the bed and stare at the ceiling thinking. There is often a lot to think about at times like this, rare as they might be.

I hear her taking a shower. I climb in the tub and put my ear to the tiles and listen to her humming.

It may not be much, but it's something. I open my travel bag, take out Dostoyevsky's *Crime and Punishment*, and weigh it carefully in my hand. The bullets had been real, I could've cashed out of the game tonight. I flip through the book and read a few lines aloud, and then I turn on the television and order a porno flick. *Zypho: the Post-modern Neo-expressionistic Morality Play* is already taking shape in my mind, but I need a third act with some real heat.

EVERYTHING THAT YOU WANT
by C.D. Formetta
(translation by Maxim Jakubowski)

If you are born a slave, you will also die a slave.

Don't listen to anyone who says otherwise, and don't believe those who say they spend their time ordering others around, but who in private prefer to be dominated. They are lying to you.

Slavery is not a choice, and neither is it a lifestyle. Or a set of clothes you only wear a few hours every day. Slavery is both a sentence and a virtue. It's a punishment one must be proud to earn. It is the pain of brutal intercourse that draws you to pleasure, it's the voice of your Master ordering you to do something and the mark of his fingertips searching between your legs until it hurts. But pain is also a sweeter form of pleasure.

I was born a slave thirty-five years ago. My parents shaped my will into the virtues of obedience. They always chose for me, first my friends, then university, and of course the young men I was allowed to go out with, then the husband I wed. I did everything according to their will, without ever complaining. I graduated in architecture, frequented the best families, only went out with serious and respectable young men, and finally I married Alberto.

I married him and almost immediately betrayed him.

You might say that's a contradiction in terms, an awful form of rebellion, but it defined me as a slave. Or maybe not.

But it was no rebellion, because Alberto is not my Master, and never was.

Alberto doesn't really know who I am. He looks at me and only sees his adorable wife, a woman to be looked after, treated with respect.

I am aware I am not worthy of his respect.

I forget the roast in the oven, only remember to take it out when it's badly burned and I say nothing to him about it. I drive the car against a lamppost, and he stays calm. He forgives me.

At least once I would like Alberto to slap me. Just once would I like to receive the punishment I deserve. If Alberto had somehow been my Master, he would already have dragged into the room and ripped my night-dress off my back, thrown it to the ground and left me there, naked and humiliated before his eyes. He would beat me just because he felt like doing so, pinched my nipples until the pain roared.

Had Alberto somehow become my Master, I would have been his faithful slave, forever. But Alberto doesn't have the character, or the necessary inner strength to impose himself and dominate me. Alberto always takes a shower before he makes love because he is afraid his smell will bother me, and he sleeps wearing a cotton vest because he has allergies, suffers from dermatitis and scratches himself all night.

Alberto is a discreet and well educated husband, But he is not my true Master.

My Master is another.

I met Franco two years back, on the occasion of a work dinner.

We were introduced and quickly discovered how much we had in common, his work as an architect, his passion for French cinema, a fond affection for jazz. Most of all we were brought together by the discovery of these similarities. We completed each other.

He was a dominant; that was obvious at first glance, just watching the way he moved and spoke. His gestures were precise and secure, he never hesitated or stumbled. His words did not make demands, they just affirmed the certitude of his will. And his answers obviously precluded any comeback.

Franco was born to command, and I was consumed inside by

the will to obey him. Together we formed a perfect combination.

We chatted all evening about everything and nothing, our conversation full of banalities, clichés, maybe so as not to provide any suspicion to the other guests.

Following the dinner, Franco offered to walk me back home, and no one else objected. I had drunk, but not too much, but I pretended I had, so that his offer did not sound unusual. It was the first of many times I would say yes to Franco.

We had almost reached my house, when Franco changed his mind.

"Come with me," he said.

"Yes," I replied.

That night, Franco became my Master.

Franco's house was big and luxurious. It was the house of a well-to-do man who had no problems showing off how rich he was. It was built on two levels, and you entered it through a lounge, and the bedroom could only be reached through a flight of stairs.

"Go up," he ordered. "I want to see how you move."

I obeyed. I was wearing a black evening dress which clung tightly to my hips, and left much of my legs uncovered. As I slowly walked up the narrow stairs I knew that his eyes were examining my body. He kept on watching me as I stood in his room, and I felt short of breath.

"You slip into a total stranger's bedroom, and you say nothing?" he asked me. "I could be a madman, a maniac. I could do anything to you, even kill you. You wouldn't be able to escape, there's nowhere here to hide yourself."

I didn't know what to think. I was frightened and he was in charge.

"Are you afraid of me?"

"Yes," I said. And his hand slid between my legs.

"Are you afraid of me?" Franco repeated, while his finger slipped into my cunt and explored my insides like a hook drilling through bait. "Are you afraid of me?"

"Yes," I moaned. Then Franco pulled his hand away and caressed my cheeks. His fingers were still wet from me.

"Liar."

He made me stretch out on the bed and slowly undressed me. He enjoyed witnessing my lack of resistance, seeing that I would allow Him to do whatever he wished to me.

"Franco..." I hesitantly said. But he put his hand against my mouth.

"Stay quiet," he said. "I don't want you to say my name."

He then unbuttoned his shirt, slipped out of his trousers and stood there, by the bed, facing me naked.

"Look at me,"

And I looked. The Master was short and thin, with his cock out of all proportion with the rest of his body. His arms were covered by short, curly black hair, all the way down from his shoulders. I didn't find his body pleasant. However I couldn't take my eyes off Him.

Now, the Master wanted to see me better.

"Open your legs."

Once again I was obedient and yielded.

"More, I said!"

The Master took hold of my ankles and forcefully pushed my legs wide apart, lowered his eyes and began examining me in full detail.

"You're tight," he said. "Hasn't your husband yet used you thoroughly?"

"I didn't quite understand what he was on about until the moment he violently slammed himself into me.

"Your husband doesn't know how to fuck you, I see."

No, I wanted to scream. My husband doesn't know what to do with me, he doesn't understand that I have no need for kisses, or embraces. Not even a caress is necessary. Only the hands of my Master forcing my legs wide, and his cock travelling so deep inside me, ripping me open like a piece of meat, sundering my life apart.

One part of my life was with Alberto and his romantic and repetitive attentions. My other life was fully devoted to my Master. From today onwards, with Him, i would travel this new road.

That evening, the Master allowed me to leave. But had he asked me to stay there, in his bed, all night long, I would have accepted, as I would have also agreed to return to him the following day, and again the day after. Every time He desired me, I would grant his desire.

Many believe that slavery is violence, torture, a simple affair of whips and chains, but that's not the way it is. *Real* slavery is so much more complicated.

Slavery is most of all a mental attitude. It means to be aware of one's own limits and understand that if you are not strong enough to be in charge, you should be strong enough to accept the authority of someone who is.

My Master has no need to jail me, to gag me or have me wear a hood of black latex. These are theatrical props, accessories for bourgeois couples seeking a mildly transgressive evening.

Slavery is being a thing, just an object for another's pleasure with no questions asked, unconditionally.

The Master calls me to join him, and i run to Him. The Master demands I not touch him, that I do not say his name, and I stay spread-eagled on the bed without moving, utterly silent, while He is free to do anything he wishes.

When we are together, the Master knows I am no longer a person. In those moments, I am just a body, of which he will dispose whenever he will.

I go along with all his demands.

One night, my Master insisted on massaging my back. He had done so on other occasions, and I knew what he wanted of me. I turned onto my stomach and allowed him to proceed. I felt very tender. He sprayed some perfumed oil over my body and began to stroke me with slow and light movements, first my back, then my shoulders, and finally my legs. I could feel his fingers moving towards my pubis, barely grazing it then moving away again. Nothing else happened that night. It entertained him to excite me this way, bringing me close to pleasure and then denying it. It made him feel even more strong and powerful. And this did not make me angry, neither did I return home straight afterwards to ask my husband to make love to me so as to calm my fever down, or to take a cold bath or shower that would have helped me think less of Him, to desire Him less. I knew that I must remain this way, hot

and quivering, until the time came for our next encounter. This is
what the Master expected of me, and I would never deceive him.
ever.

That night, my Master continued to touch me until my body
could not bear it any more and my patience was strung out like a
bow, and he masturbated in my presence while I was required to
watch, and I envied him this moment of release because He was
free to do what he wanted. Only He had the power to give and
take.

There were other times. And on every occasion, the Master
made the same mistake.

It's not that I really envied him, there was no reason to. He
gave me everything that I wanted, everything that I ever needed.
He provided me with rules, orders, tasks to complete before his
return. I kept my mind occupied and distant from my simpering
conjugal life, outwardly perfect and harmonic, but in truth so dull
and lifeless. Motionless on the bed, with my Master taking care of
me, I was happy. I finally had everything I wanted, everything I
had ever dreamed of.

I loved him. I loved my Master with blind and absolute
devotion. I loved him so much it became impossible not to express
it in my emotions.

"You are everything I want," I said to him.

I felt him stiffen. Unexpectedly, the Master moved his hands
away from me and became distant. He looked at me with a new
expression on his face, his eyes were faraway. He was angry.

"Who said you could even *want something*?" he shouted. "You
do not have my permission to desire me or any one else. You no
longer have desires, you no longer have any will."

I had disappointed him. I had understood nothing.

I understood that soon the Master would get rid of me.

Once again, I find myself travelling down a one way road,
living a one way life. The Master no longer summons me, and I do
not attempt to make contact with Him. I know that should I do so
I would anger him even more. I had no news from him for a long,
unending period, but I allowed the weeks, the months to go by,
hoping that somehow it would soothe the pain slightly.

I have withstood the temptation to take other lovers or new masters. I finally accepted Alberto's proposal to go out on a Saturday to do the shopping together, like so many of the contented couples in this city. It was then I saw him. Him, my Master.

He was entering a shop in the center of town with a new young girl by his side. He gallantly held the door open for her, allowing her to enter first, then together they began to look at the evening dresses. It was then the young woman became angry. She raised her voice and stated that she wanted the leather miniskirt and the ankle boots, that she could no longer walk about in her present long skirt that made her look like a middle-aged woman. My Master tried to excuse her, tried to take hold of her hands, but she resisted him. The young girl was determined to cause a public scene. She turned and left my Master standing there in the middle of the store and walked out, muttering that she preferred to walk home on foot. It was only then that I began to understand what my eyes had just witnessed.

My Master was no longer my Master, in fact he was no longer the master of anything. He was only one of the many men who had chosen the wrong toy. A common mistake, particularly in a relationship of this kind, so different from ours. A relationship in which there were no similarities, only a gap, a distance that time would only make worse.

In fact, that young girl couldn't have been much more than twenty years old,

And my Master, on the other hand, would be forty next week.

FOUR ON THE FLOOR
by Alison Tyler

We weren't very nice about it. That was the surprising part. I expected the cliche of scented oils and the gilded candlelight ambiance and the slippery limbs entwined. But how we acted afterwards was unforseen. Alone together, reliving the night, Sam and I were truly cruel. And here I was, operating under a false impression for so many years.

You see, I always thought I was a nice girl.

Others recalling the experience might focus on the way Sheila's grayblue eyes had lit up when I'd pressed my mouth to her freshly shaved pussy, or the look on her husband Richard's craggy but handsome face as he started to slowly stroke his long, uncut cock. But not this girl. The best part of the evening for me was the laughter with Sam afterwards, giggling all the way home about the freaks we'd spent the evening with. The freaks we'd just fucked.

They were decades older than us, and richer by far, and they'd run a charming ad at the back of the Pink Section of the *SF Chronicle*. Filled with dizzy anticipation, we met for drinks, to check out the chemistry factor. Sizing up potential fuck partners is a heady business. Nobody else in the trendy after-work bar knew that we were responding to a personal. Not the cute curly-haired bartender. Not the female executives lined up against the wall like pretty maids all in a row. The thought of what we were actually there for made me giddy with excitement, and desire showed rather brightly in my dark eyes.

The woman said I was pretty. Her husband agreed with an anxious nod. All evening long, they looked at me rather than Sam, and I knew why. Sam is tough. He has short, razor-cut hair and a gingery goatee. If you were to meet him in a back alley, you'd offer him your wallet in a heartbeat. You'd beg him to take it, the way I beg him to take things from me every night.

The couple didn't understand Sam. So they talked to me instead.

"So pretty," the woman repeated. "Like Snow White."

I grinned and drank my Cosmo, then licked my cherry-glossed lips in the sexiest manner I could manage, leaving the tip of my tongue in the corner of my mouth for one second too long. Iridescent sparkles lit-up my long dark hair. Multicolored body glitter decorated my pale skin. I wore serpentine black leather pants and a white baby-T with the word SINNER screaming across the chest in deep scarlet. There was an unspoken emphasis on how young I was in comparison to the woman. She was holding firm in her mid-forties, while I was just barely getting used to being in my early twenties. Her entire attitude was both calculating and clearly at ease, obvious in the way she held court in our booth, in the way she ordered from the waiter without even looking up.

"Two Kettle-One Martinis, another Cosmo, another Pilsner."

I was her opposite, bouncy and ready, a playful puppy tugging on a leash. More than that, I was bold from how much they wanted us, and I was wet from how much I wanted Sam. When he put one firm hand on my thigh under the table, I nearly swooned against him. We'd be ripping our clothes off each other in hours.

After drinking away the evening, we made a real date with the rich couple for the following weekend, a date at their place, where they promised to show us their sunken hot tub, wrap-around deck, and panoramic view of the city. In cultured voices, they bragged to us about the gold records from his music-producing days, and her collection of antique Viennese perfume bottles accumulated with the assistance of Ebay. But although I listened politely, I didn't care about their money or what it could buy. All I wanted was all Sam wanted which was simple: four on the floor.

We had done the act already, nearly a year before, with a lower class duo Sam found for us on the internet. The woman was thirty-eight, the man twenty-six. They'd been together for two years, and had wanted to sample another couple as a way of enhancing their already wild sex life. After dinner at a local pizzeria, and two bottles of cheap red wine, Pamela and I retreated to the ladies' room to show each other our tattoos. Hers was a dazzling fuchsia strawberry poised right below her bikini line. When she lifted her white dress, I saw that not only was she pantyless, but that she'd been very recently spanked. She blushed becomingly as I admired her glowing red rear cheeks, where lines from Andy's belt still glowed in stark relief against her coppery skin.

"He gave me what-for in the parking lot," she confessed. "Told me that he wanted me to behave during dinner."

"What would he think of this?" I asked, stroking her still-warm ass with the open palm of my hand.

"I think he'd approve," she grinned.

I gave her a light slap on her tender skin, and she turned around and caught me in a quick embrace, lifting my dress slowly so that she could see my own ink.

Teasingly, I turned to show her the cherries on my lower back, then pulled down my bikinis to reveal the blue rose riding on my hip. She traced my designs with the tips of her fingers, and I felt as if I were falling. Her touch was so light, so gentle, and in moments we started French-kissing, right there in the women's room at Formico's, while I could only imagine what the men were doing. Speaking of macho topics to one another, sports and the recent war, while growing harder and harder as they waited for us to return to the red-and-white checked table.

Sam and I followed the duo to their Redwood City apartment, and into their tiny living room, overshadowed by a huge-screen TV and a brown faux-leather sofa. Pamela had her tongue in my asshole before my navy blue sleeveless dress was all the way off, and my mouth was on Andy's mammoth cock before he could kick off his battered black motorcycle boots.

The TV stayed on the whole time we were there. Muted, but on. We had crazy sex right on the caramel-colored shag rug in front of it, while heavy metal bands played for us in silence. It was like doing it on stage with Guns & Roses. Surreal, but not a turn-off.

I remember a lot of wetness—her mouth, his mouth, her pussy. I remember Sam leaning against the wood-paneled wall at one point in the evening and watching, just watching the three of us entwined, the TV-glow flickering over us, my slim body stretched out between our new lovers. I felt beloved as their fingers stroked me, as they took turns tasting me, splitting my legs as wide as possible and getting in between. I held my arms over my head and Sam bent down and gripped my wrists tight while Pamela licked at me like a pussycat at a saucer of milk.

Scenes flowed through the night, lubricated by our red-wine daze, and we moved easily from one position to another. Pamela bent on her knees at Sam's feet and brought her mouth to his cock. I worked Andy, bobbing up and down, and after he came for the first time, I moved over to Pamela's side, so we could take turns drinking from Sam. I was reeling with the wonder of it. The illusion that anything was possible. Any position, any desire.

"You like that?" Andy asked when I returned to his side, pointing to Pamela as she sucked off my husband. "You like watching?"

I nodded.

"What else do you like?"

"I like that you spanked her," I confessed in a soft voice.

"Ah," he smiled. "So you're a bad girl, too."

My blush told him all he needed to know, and soon I was upended over his sturdy lap, and the erotic clapping sounds of a bare-ass spanking rang through the room. Andy punished me to perfection, not letting up when I started to cry and squirm, making me earn the pleasure that flooded through me. Sam filled Pamela's mouth while watching another man tan my hide.

Andy was a true sadist, which I could appreciate. He had a pair of shiny orange-handled pliers which he used like a magician on his girlfriend's teacup tits. She didn't cry or scream; she moaned. He twisted the pliers harder, and her green eyes took on a vibrant glow, as if she'd found some deep hidden secret within herself, and as if that secret gave her power. Andy told us stories of how he liked to spank her with his hand or belt or paddle. Sometimes he used a wooden ruler. Sometimes he used whatever was nearby. He told us detailed stories of how he fucked her up the ass, how he made her bend over and part her cheeks for him, holding herself open as wide as possible, and begging him for it. He liked to lube her up good, and then pour a handful of K-Y into his fist and pump his cock once or twice before taking her. The size of his cock in her backdoor would often make her cry, but it was a good sort of cry, he explained. Pain and pleasure were entwined in everything they did. Andy's stories made me more excited, and we kept up our games all night long, screwing on stage with the long-haired boys in the bands.

Sam and I had fun with that couple, and we didn't laugh afterwards. We fucked. Not like bunnies, which are cute and soft and sweet. We fucked like us. Hard and raw and all the time. Sam's large hand slapped down on my ass, connecting over and over as he relived the night. "You little cock slut," he said, his voice gravelly and low. "Your mouth was all hungry for him. You couldn't get enough." I would be red and sore after our sessions, and I relished every mark, every pale plum-colored bruise, every memory. The night was fuel for a year's worth of fantasies. We got precisely what we wanted, even though we never saw them again, because the woman turned out to be mildly insane. She called and called after our one-night stand. She emailed that she was in love with me, that she was desperate to see me. But Sam and I didn't want love. We wanted something much less involved but much more momentarily intense: four on the floor.

With Sheila and Richard, we got a great deal more than we bargained for. A gourmet dinner—delivered by a local party service—that dragged on for hours. A tour of their two-story house and their walk-in closets. Close-up views of their his and-hers Armanis. We received an indepth explanation of how their pure pedigreed dogs, who were busy in the corner of the living room chewing on pigs' ears, had been "de-barked." Their voice boxes were removed, which had caused the dogs so much trauma, the pets were now on puppy-Prozac.

These appearance-obsessed people were the ones we were about to have sex with. I had a difficult time picturing it. Yes, she was attractive, although "cool" was a better word. Yes, I liked how distinguished he looked in his open-necked crisp white shirt and pressed khakis with the ironed creased down the center. He was so different from Sam with his faded Levis and dangling silver wallet chain. But they were trying to win us over, and somehow that made me feel hard and bristly inside. Didn't stop us from getting busy, though—from choosing a spot far way from those demented dogs and peeling our clothes off. Richard didn't fuck me. He sat nearby and stroked my sleek dark hair out of my eyes and said he wanted to watch. Sheila had on a black velvet catsuit, and she stripped it off with one practiced move and was naked, her platinum hair rippling over her shoulders, her body gleaming chestnut in the candlelight. She stood for a moment, holding the pose, waiting for applause or flashbulbs.

Sam took his cue from Richard at first, backing away, watching while Sheila courted me. Sheila had obviously done this before. She strode to my side and helped to undress me. She cooed softly, admiringly, as she undid my bra and pulled it free, as she slid my satin dove-gray panties down my thighs. Her fingers inspected me all over, as if she checking to see that a purchase she'd made was acceptable. She kissed wetly into the hollow of my neck and caressed my breasts with her long, delicate fingers, tweaking my rosy nipples just so to make them erect. Then she spread me out on the luxurious multi-colored living room rug and started to kiss along the basin of my belly. I had one second to wonder why it is that menages never take place in beds before I sighed and arched my back, parted my legs for her, closed my eyes. She turned her body, lowered herself on me, let me taste her.

Everything about her body felt cool, like polished foil. Her skin. Her lips. Her tangy juices when they flooded out to meet my tongue. We sixty-nined for the men, and for a moment, I was won over. I was fine, alert and happy. With my mouth on the older woman's pussy, and my hands stroking her perfect silky body, I lost myself in momentary bliss. She was exotically perfumed, a scent I didn't recognize but knew must have been imported from Europe. She even tasted expensive. But sex levels out any playing field. I might only have been able to afford CoverGirl dimestore cosmetics rather than Neiman-Marcus special blends, but I could find her swollen clit easily, and that's all that mattered. I teased it out from between her perfectly shaved pussy lips. I sucked hard, and then used my tongue to trace ring around the rosy.

When I felt Sam's eyes on me, I turned my head to look at him. He gave me a wink, as if to let me know that he approved, and then he nodded forward with his head for me to continue. I could already hear his voice in my head, "You liked your mouth all glossy with pussy juices, didn't you, girl? You liked the way she tasted, all slippery and wet?

But then Sheila started to direct, positioning my body on all fours, before grabbing a carved wooden box from under the coffee table and pulling out a variety of sex toys. This wasn't like Andy lifting his pliers off the oval-shaped coffee table, an unexpected turn-on. This was planned; I could tell. We had been carefully chosen to star in a pre-written fantasy of Sheila's. A fantasy in which she was the star and I was her assistant, her underling, her protege. And even as she buckled on the thick, pink strap-on, I felt myself withdraw.

Still, we fucked.

She took me from behind, and she held tightly onto my long black hair, and rode me. Her well-manicured fingertips gripped firmly near the base of my scalp, holding me in place. Sam stared into my eyes as I was pounded by this icy woman, and then he came close, his cock out, and placed the very head on my full bottom lip. I heard Sheila hiss something—Sam was taking charge and she didn't like it. But she also didn't know Sam. Sam would have none of her noise, the way she would have none from her dogs. He fucked my mouth fiercely while she fucked my cunt, and while Richard, silent and somewhere off inside himself, tugged on his dick and watched us all.

Sheila had oils that she spread on me with the finesse of a masseuse, and soon we were drippy and glistening in the golden light. She had sturdy metal nipple clamps and assorted colorful dildos, vibrating devices and butt plugs. She arrayed her collection and went to work. And Sam let it all happen. This was far different, and far less spontaneous, from our experience with Pamela and

Andy, but we'd use it. We'd go with it. There were four of us, after all, and we were there.

I came when she oiled me up between my rear cheeks and slowly slipped in a petal-pink butt plug, her knowing fingers working between my thighs to tickle my clit as she filled my ass with the toy. I came again when Sam jacked himself hard and let loose in my mouth, filling me up with his cream as Sheila fucked me from behind. I jammed my own fingers between my legs, working my own clit to come a final time when Richard, so distant, lowered his head and shuddered, his body wracked with tremors as he climaxed a white fountain up onto his hard belly.

But in the car at 2 a.m., on the way home, still reeking of imported essential oils, still throbbing from the poundings I'd taken, I started to giggle. And then Sam started to laugh out loud.

"Voice boxes removed," he said, shaking his head as he drove along the empty highway.

"Crazy."

"So much Armani," he snorted.

"And gold records."

"And cigars."

"And their view."

"And their money."

And we didn't see them again, even though they called for weeks afterwards. Even though they fell a little bit in love with us, as had Pamela and Andy. Because Sam and I weren't looking for love. We had plenty of that. We were looking for one thing only. And somehow I was sure that we'd find it again once I placed a personal ad of our own:

Happily married twosome seeks similar couple for debauchery. For intensity. For four on the floor.

GAME NIGHT
by Cate Robertson

Before she showered, he placed several wrapped packages on the bed.

"Wear these."

He opened her robe and with his fingernail, slowly incised a long, narrow inverted triangle on her mound. "Shave like this." He went out.

She showered before unwrapping the gifts. That gave her time to imagine what he'd given her. Then, still damp, she hurried to open the presents. Wrapped in gold-veined pink tissue were tiny black things: lace bra, garter belt, sheer stockings, new lipstick, and a tiny vial of Surrender. All her favorites. It was their turn this month to host Game Night, and the first rule flickered in her mind.

Rule #1 The slave shall present as the master dictates.

No thong. Had he forgotten it? She fished in her drawer for his favorite—smooth black with a deep-dip front—then tied on her black silk robe, and headed downstairs.

The girls were chattering behind the closed door in the family room—for tonight, the slave den. They would be watching a chick flick, ordering in Chinese or Thai, gossiping, drinking wine and coolers, waiting for the hockey game to end. Tonight, she was not permitted to speak to them, nor would she be joining them later.

But they would all be dressed much as she was.

She entered the living room right on cue. The theme music for the hockey game was just beginning. The room was illuminated only by the big screen TV.

He smiled. "We need some beers."

Rule #4 The guest masters shall watch the entire game with the host master, attended by his slave.

Sean, Ross, Drew, Mike, and him. All of them partners at the firm. Focused on the big screen, they passed comments on the game, ignoring her as she served cold beers, chips, and pretzels. He motioned to her. "Untie that. And put out some olives."

As she returned with the platter, her robe floating open, he scowled. "What the fuck—"

The chatting stopped. Her blood ran cold. "Come here, " he said. They were all watching her.

He hooked his finger into the front of the thong. "You had no permission to wear this." He took out a pocketknife, flicked open the blade. He pulled the fabric tight. The blade flashed, sliced through one side, then the other. She flinched.

Roughly, he tugged the slashed thong from between her legs and tossed it to Mike. They passed it around, chuckling, joking about its wetness. Her wetness. Drew put it to his face and inhaled, sighing teasingly.

"Verdict?" he demanded of her.

She swallowed and said, "Guilty."

He said, "Penalty One."

They watched her expectantly.

Penalty One: If a robe is worn, the slave shall remove it.

She dropped it to the floor and stood before them in bra and gartered stockings. Mike gave a low wolf-whistle. Drew muttered, "Beautiful shave."

He got up and moved behind her, kissed her neck and shoulder, ran his hands into the slickness between her legs, drew her folds apart rhythmically. Eyes closed, she leaned back against him, rocked her hips, moaned. Someone grunted.

"Undo me," he said, pushing her down to her knees before him.

She looked at him pleadingly. Already? He ignored her gaze.

Rule #3 Refusal to comply with a command will result in penalty in extremis.

Rule #6 On the host night, the master shall freely enjoy his own slave's favors in front of the guest masters.

He surged out as she popped the buttons on his fly and pulled his jeans loose. The only sound in the room was the play-by-play.

She bent her face into him, took his hard flesh in her mouth. His hands clenched in her hair and he forced her head tight against him as he shuddered to his conclusion. Dutifully, she swallowed and licked him clean. Someone, Mike she thought, whispered, "Fuckin' Christ, Steve." There was restless stirring, deep breathing, a fist or two slapping quietly.

The bell rang to end the first period.

She washed her hands and face before arranging the appetizers—devilled eggs, marinated mussels, crab cakes in hot sauce. When the second period started, he instructed her to sit astride each guest master's lap and hand feed each one the hors d'oeuvres of his choice.

Rule #8 The guest masters may compliment and encourage the host's slave. They shall not touch her.

Obviously huge and rigid in their pants, they made manful attempts at small talk as she went around. She knew them all, intimately, from previous Game Nights, of course, but she particularly liked Sean. He moved his thigh under her and she left a wet spot on the leg of his khakis.

Ross said, "Angela, you look fucking gorgeous tonight."

Drew sidestepped the rule and lipped her finger. "Your crab cakes are the best, darling."

Settling onto Mike's lap, she lost her balance with the platter, and his arm went round her waist, a brief touch to steady her.

"Whoa, sweetheart. Sorry, Steve. Reflex." He shrugged.

"That's okay, man. It's not devilled eggs you want in your lap, is it?"

They laughed.

She served him last. He made her straddle him while she fed him. When the platter was empty, he gripped her ass, pulled her closer, slipped his fingers between her legs. The cursory chatter behind fell silent. She knew none of them were watching the game now.

He unclasped the bra, dropped it. Someone, Drew maybe, sighed. He sucked until her nipples were hard. His hand worked in her pussy. She squirmed, arched her back, tossed her head back. Ross groaned, "Jesus, let her have it."

He dropped his hands and leaned back in the chair. He didn't say a word. He didn't have to. She knew her duty. Obediently, she spread his shirt and jeans open, pressed herself quivering down onto him. At first he grasped her shoulders to push her down firmly, but towards the end, he was clutching her hips, driving into her. Behind her, she dimly heard heavy panting, repeated gasps of "Fuck."

The second period ended.

During the third period, she served her specialty, homemade pizza with a cheese-stuffed crust and the works. He had her cut and serve each piece individually from the low coffee table. She was bending over and moving among them, flushed and pendulous.

Then he asked, "Why isn't there any hot sausage on this?"

Her nipples pricked hard as a shiver swept up her spine. She said, "They didn't have any at the store this week."

"And you dare to serve me pizza without hot sausage? You disobey a standing order?"

Ross muttered, "Uh-oh."

Drew said, "You're fucking in for it now, baby."

He said, "I think you know the verdict for blatant disobedience of standing orders."

She nodded and bowed her head. "Guilty."

He declared, "Penalty Four."

Sean whispered, "Yes!" They loved administering Penalty Four. She swallowed hard.

Penalty Four: The buttocks shall be beaten according to the table of punishments below.

She had memorized the table of punishments. She knew the rules inside out, as he did. As they all did. After all, they had created Game Night together, as a group. Everyone had had a say in the construction of the game. Each couple had personally evaluated and endorsed in writing every single detail, every rule and every penalty. Penalty Four included a list of instruments with the number of blows allowed for each, ranging from twelve for "open hand" to two for "riding crop."

He stood up and pulled his stuffed chair out into the middle of the room, revealing a chest behind it. This contained the instruments of punishment.

He ran a finger inside the band of her garter belt and drew her closer. "Get in position."

She bent over the plush back of the chair, her flesh straining against the black garters. He stroked her ass almost tenderly and she shuddered. She was trying hard to focus on the calculations. If they all chose open hand, she was in for sixty hard smacks. But there were also belts and switches of various materials, weight, and flexibility. They had all been carefully evaluated by the whole group.

Someone would be sure to choose the riding crop.

No one ever held back. Penalty Four beatings were always full-force.

She was pulsing madly inside.

He did not tie her to the chair. He left her wrists and ankles unbound. Had he forgotten? He was kneading her ass hard now, spreading her cheeks, warming her up. Her hips rocked gently and she pressed her face into the upholstery, ready for it.

They stood around her with their beers, joking and taking turns selecting their instruments. Penalty Four was a favorite, so they took their time, discussing the relative merits of each instrument and taking practice swoops through the air to startle her. Teasing her was part of the fun.

"This'll make her good and red, man."

"She loves that one. She loves it when you give her stripes."

"Look, no-one's used this for a while. This stings. Really hot."

Finally they were ready. Each stepped up to her in turn. Open hand always went first. Ross, twelve blows. Then Sean, quarter-inch birch sapling, eight blows. Drew, two-inch belt, four blows. Mike, eighth-inch nylon rope, six blows. The room resounded with the measured commotion of beating, and she knew that by now, the girls would be silent, counting the blows, hardly daring to breathe, squirming and wet.

She could never decide which was more breathtaking—the searing pain or her ferocious arousal.

When his turn came, he rummaged in the box, found what he sought. She felt him take a few practice strokes, lightly touching her ass to test the angle and distance. Ross made a joke about teeing off. Then came the heavy swoop of the crop, descending. Her flesh blazed. Involuntarily she cried out. One.

Two.

Three times. Not permitted!

"Stop!" She pushed herself up and faced him, flushed and shaking. "That was three."

Rule #10 Slaves shall not contradict the master.

Rule #13 Slaves shall remain in position until released by the master.

Mike said, "Uh-oh."

Drew hummed the theme from *Jaws*. Then they all fell silent. The game was tied up in the final minutes but no one was paying attention to it now.

Rule #15 Breaking two rules at once shall result in automatic penalty in extremis.

She suddenly realized his trick. He had not bound her because he had wagered, correctly, that she would jump up in protest. He had arranged it so that she would break two rules at once.

He smiled victoriously. "One count of contradiction. One count of leaving the position without permission. Verdict on both counts?"

She glared at him, flushed and trembling. "Not guilty. You manipulated me." Someone whistled.

He pronounced the penalty coolly. "For breaking two rules at once, and for further defiance of rules duly agreed to by this group, penalty in extremis."

The buzzer rang to end the game. Someone immediately clicked off the set. The only sound she could hear in the room now was her own heart, hammering in her throat.

Rule #19 Penalty in extremis shall be delivered privately by

the master.

They were all getting up now, stretching, rubbing themselves in anticipation. Drew nudged him with a grin. "Don't do anything I wouldn't do, man."

Sean added, "Give her a lick for me." Laughing, they trooped out.

Game Night group activity:

At the end of the third period, the guest masters shall be served by the guest slaves in a group, in the slave den. No exclusions or refusals are allowed. Slaves shall copulate with masters, as commanded, in couples or in any combination of masters and slaves. This activity may continue as long as any master desires.

From the family room issued a scuffling confusion of movement and a chorus of excited squeals, soon muffled or transformed into moans of pleasure— and of agony. The group activity was underway.

Not for her, not for him. Not tonight.

Tonight, he was administering penalty in extremis. He upended her over the chair again. This time he tied her firmly into position, wrists to the front legs of the chair, ankles to the back, on her toes, legs splayed wide with her red-striped buttocks slightly parted.

From behind, his fingers found her swollen clit and his thumb slipped inside her. He massaged her slowly and vigorously until she lurched, groaning, against her bonds. Then he placed both hands on her burning cheeks and drew them apart, wider and wider, until she thought she would split in two and the rush of cold air into her slick crevice made her blood boil with anticipation and dread. She closed her eyes and braced herself for the glide of his tongue up her smoothly-waxed crack. Again. Oh, again. Then, right there, the coaxing, circling probe of a fingertip, the patient pulse of a stiffened tongue-tip.

Abruptly, in an instant, her delicate core of resistance gave way. She felt her flesh unclench and relax into openness and she became one molten nerve. She gasped, or shouted, or maybe it was him, or both of them.

She startled at the rip of his zipper.

In the next instant, he would transfix her like a butterfly

struggling against the penetrating steel. He would propel her in extremis, in slow moaning motion, headfirst, upwards through gathering darkness to the blinding brink of delirium, millimeter by singing, screaming, soaring millimeter.

Rule #20 The game is only over when the master—and slave—are satisfied.

HIS JUST REWARDS
by Rachel Kramer Bussel

"Hello?"

"Good, I'm glad you're home. I'm coming over in five minutes. Turn off your TV or computer or whatever else you have on. When I get there, I want you to be completely naked and ready for me. I'll let you know what to do when I get there. Okay?" I snap this out in my best commanding tone, never letting on that I'm shaking and nervous. I say this like I talk this way all the time, even though so far I've only hinted at what a bitch I can be. I have a clear sense of direction and purpose, have summoned all my power for one final, explosive encounter that will only work if I play it cool.

I arrive a few minutes later and knock briskly on the door. He opens it naked but with sandals on. I march right in, pushing past him, pulling Karla into the room after me, just daring him to ask me who she is or what she's doing here. Maybe he knows, maybe he doesn't, but it's not my problem.

"What are those doing on your feet?" I ask disdainfully, pointing at the shoes. I don't wait for him to respond before continuing, "Take those shoes off and get down on your knees." Anticipating his protests about the dusty floor, I bark, "Don't argue, just do it!"

I hand Karla the bag and signal to her to fish out the riding crop I've packed specifically for this occasion. I feel much bigger

than my 5'2" height, and not just because of the severe black heels
I'm wearing. This is good because he's big and strapping and I
need all of my willpower to go through with this. When he's on
the floor, I nudge him with my foot, tapping his ass and telling
him to start crawling. We follow him as he leads us to his office.
"Now get up."

He keeps looking at me with those puppy-dog eyes that beg
me to pet and kiss and coddle him, to give him a hint of the affection
he's come to crave from me. But affection isn't a one-sided
transaction, and I have only so much to give without getting what
I require in return. I've been waiting for his side of the bargain, his
compliance with my very simple demand, a question in search of
an answer, and so far he hasn't come close. It's time to teach him a
lesson.

He sits in the chair, and I secure his ankles to the chair's legs,
then wrap bondage tape around his chest and knees, in enough
places so that I'm confident that he's secured. I want to bind his
wrists but settle for only one, leaving the other free, not because I
want him to use it, but to tempt him into committing acts I'll have
to punish him for later. Karla senses that I don't need her help and
goes off to the adjoining bedroom to wait for me.

"Even though I know you want to be the best little boy you
can be and obey all of my commands to the letter, I'm a little worried
that you're going to try to talk to me or scream or make noise that
will distract me from fucking Karla. So I'm just going to have to
tape your mouth to prevent you from even attempting anything
like that."

I pull off a length of the shiny red tape and fasten it over his
mouth. I slap his cheeks lightly, one and then the other, and then,
because it feels so good, again. His cheeks take on rosy tone. "You
look good like that. Don't you agree?" I ask in a babying tone as I
pinch his cheek, hard. He nods, and I smile in response.

As I step back to survey my handiwork, he looks at me
beseechingly. I bring my hand forward and caress his cheek. "Am
I supposed to feel sorry for you, all alone out here with only a
video to keep you company, turned around so you can't see us all
naked and fucking each other? Have you ever seen two girls

together? I bet you haven't, but the thought of it turns you on. I bet you'd like to watch, like to see her sucking on my nipples and me licking her pussy, like to see me lay her across my lap and spank her."

I look down and notice his cock twitching from his restrained lap, and I can't resist a brief stroke over his hardness. "Not that I know for sure what you're into, since you've been a bit reticent with that information, haven't you? But on this count I know I'm right. You *would* like that a lot, wouldn't you?"

He nods.

"Well, you'll just have to guess what we're doing, though if you're lucky you might get to hear her scream a little bit. But you're not gonna see any of it. I did bring this video to keep you company, and I selected it just for you."

As I put the cassette in the VCR and queue it up, I'm reminded of my babysitting days, when a cartoon was all it took to pacify a screaming, whiny child. This video is for adults only, but it will hopefully have the same effect. "Now, I'm just going to get you settled in here and leave you with this video, and I want you to be good and quiet and pay attention. There'll be no closing your eyes and definitely no stroking your cock. Like I said, I picked this video especially for you because I think there are some good lessons you can learn about what it means to be a good boy and respond to orders and you'll see in it what happens when you don't. I want you to watch carefully what kinds of punishments these mean mistresses dish out, because that should give you a little taste of what's in store for you when I get back."

I watch as his eyes fixate on the image of a large man strung upside down from the ceiling of a dungeon, while two scantily clad, sexy women beat and torture him. A quick glance at his cock shows me that it at least is reacting positively to the images on the screen. I don't dare give away the fact that the video actresses are much stricter than I could ever be, even in my imagination, but that doesn't mean I can't try my best. I pull a clothespin out of my pocket and present it to him. "There's a reason I left your hand free, and it's not so you can play with your cock. It's for this. You can put it anywhere on your body that you want to, but when I come back I want to see it attached to you, *somewhere*. Otherwise I'll have the pleasure of clamping it somewhere very painful myself. Got that?"

I stand in front of him, blocking his view, daring him to try to twist to watch the TV around me, or otherwise stare right at my bulging breasts. My eyes bore into his, wondering if he can even appreciate the emotions underlying my actions. Yes, I know he's been craving some sort of abuse from me, but he's also pissed me off to the extreme. I have to watch myself that I don't go overboard, don't take too much of my anger out on his willing skin. The babysitting analogy returns when I think of how childishly he's been acting lately, wanting all of the fun and none of the responsibilities of a real relationship. My questions go repeatedly unanswered, even though I find it hard to believe that a grown man doesn't have a response, can't articulate in words what gets him hard, what turns him on, what he wants. Women are supposed to be the mysterious, hard-to-read creatures, men as easy as saying "Fuck me." But it doesn't really work that way in the real world.

I wonder if I can hurt him enough that he will give me the verbal contact that I crave, the communication that has been missing since the earliest days of our relationship. I wonder if there will come a day where I can ask him to spin me a fantasy, to let me into his head, even if only for a moment, and he does. Sadly, I don't think that's in the cards for us, so I will take what I can get from him and move on.

"Now watch your video like a good little boy. I'm not giving you a pen to take notes, but I hope you'll remember what you've seen because I'm gonna ask you about it. I'll be in the other room, but don't expect me back until I'm good and ready. And don't even *think* about trying to escape. When the video is over you can sit there and play with your clothespin, but you're not to touch yourself and certainly not to come under any circumstances. Believe me, I'll know if you do. Got that?"

He nods again, and I walk away, filled with an energy that bursts through my whole body. I enter the bedroom and see her lying there, leafing through a magazine, and wonder if she's heard what just went on in the office. The sight of her fills me with an incredible urge to touch her, taste her, to have her and never let her go. I forget any potential awkwardness over the fact that I've been naked here with him as well. Now it's only about me and her, nobody else. I have a brief urge to close the door, even though I know that there's no way he can come in here and watch. Anyway, it doesn't matter. Whenever I'm with her—whether we're in a private bedroom or a public dance floor—it seems as if we're completely alone. I can melt into her, close my eyes and all of a sudden the other people surrounding us disappear. We are the only ones in existence, and she the only one occupying my attention.

The immature man I've just teased and taunted is nothing compared to her.

She glances up as I walk in, a slightly sheepish look on her face. Neither of us says anything, but a spark of understanding and desire fills the air. I pull her close to me and quickly undo her pants, then slide them down her thin legs. She's so small that sometimes I feel as if I'm with a doll, an otherworldly creature who is tender and delicate. And while she can be those things, she's shown me her strength and passion and durability. I don't have to treat her like a soft flower.

"What have you been doing in here? Have you been good? Were you listening to what I said to him?"

She nods, a slightly contrite look on her face tinged with just a hint of mischief. "Did you like that, Karla? Hmmm? Did you like the way I talked to him?" By now her pants are all the way off and I press the back of my hand against her panties, finding them wet and warm. "I think you did, I think you liked hearing me tease him and yell at him, didn't you?" I slide her panties to the side and stroke her, already so wet I just want to plunge right in. Every time I touch her it's new and beautiful; I could get lost in her pussy and never return to the real world. I press more firmly, stroking only the outside of her wet slit even as I feel her pushing up against me. "What was that, baby? Is there something you want from me? If there is you're gonna have to tell me what it is. You should know that, especially after all I've been through with that one out there not letting me in on his secrets. I'll move closer so you can whisper in my ear." I pick her up and position her so she's across my lap, face up, her face next to my ear and her pussy within arm's reach.

As much as I want to think that things with each of them are totally separate, that I've been conducting two equivalent relationships operating in separate spheres, inside, they have overlapped. The charge I got from tying him up, from knowing that I could do whatever I wanted to him, has bled over into my time with her. I am surprised that after all these years being told what to do, and liking it, the other side of the equation seems to fit me perfectly. My breathing quickens as she rubs up against me, her ass pressing into my lap and her face nuzzling my neck. I cup my hand over her pussy and leave it there, willing her to sit still. She does. The squirming stops and there is just silence and stillness, searching and sweet anticipation. I feel myself getting wetter as I realize that whatever is about to happen is under my control; I can go in whatever direction I want.

Just like that, with a split-second realization of power, I'm gushing. I push my two fingers into her pussy, knowing that she's ready so I don't need to warn her. I press deeper and feel her arch up against me, her head lolling back as she tries to take me in and stay in control, but she can't. I push as far as I can go, then ease out of her. She grabs my wrist and tries to push me back inside her.

"Soon, baby, soon, don't worry," I whisper in her ear.

She whimpers and tosses her head back and it's a sight to behold, her spread out before me as my personal plaything.

"Spread your legs for me, baby. There, that's good," I tell her as her legs widen and I can see all of her pretty pinkness. I have no idea if her other lovers talked to her like this. I am just getting used to figuring out what she wants and how I can give it to her.

I bring my hand upwards and then down on her pussy, softly at first, then with my fingers I keep going—tap, tap, tap—against her, knocking lightly at first, then harder as I see that she likes it. As if something inside me has taken over, and I'm in a trance, I bring my hand back and forth again and again, gaining in intensity each time. I pause for a moment, afraid that I'm going to get swept away in my actions and hurt her, but she begs me to continue. I do, slapping her cunt and then again slipping two and then three fingers inside her, all with an urgency that we can both feel; I must fuck her now or it will be too late. I push my fingers inside her, feeling for the most sensitive areas, pressing up and then to the side and almost wanting to cry with the magic of being so close to her center.

I let her lean back onto the bed and with my other hand press on her stomach and then slide lower, massaging her clit while pressing against her, covering her in my touch until she cries out and I feel her squeeze my fingers with a fierce intensity. I slowly pull out, awed by what has just happened, so fast and so furious. Awed but not shocked because it's like this every time we're together, with everything so new and raw and fresh I feel both like a wide-eyed virgin and an old woman, full of power and wisdom. I pull her towards me and hold her, get lost in her for another spell of time as we recover.

When we finally emerge, I've lost track of time. I'm sure the video is long over. I wonder if he'll have his eyes closed, or be playing with his dick, or trying to escape. But when I come out, pulling a naked Karla along behind me, he's sitting there looking very angelic, his free hand dangling by his side, appearing so casual you'd think he could almost have strung himself up because he was bored.

"So, how was the video? Did it bore you? Is that why you're just sitting here? Where's the clothespin?" I say this louder than I need to, because I can, because I like the sound of my voice and want to startle him, and because I know that for once nobody is going to tell me to lower my voice.

He produces the clothespin with his free hand.

"Why didn't you put it somewhere? If I'd known you were going to not follow my instructions, again, I'd have tied up both your wrists."

His face reddens.

"What I think I'm gonna do is give it to Karla to put on you"

I slap his face for emphasis and present the pin to Karla. I know she won't do too much damage to him, thinking she'll try a finger or other easy spot, but she surprises me and zeroes in on his right nipple. I give him a look to silence any potential protests. There are so many delicious possibilities of what I can do with him now that I wonder how I will manage to choose only one. I bend down and loosen his ankles from their bonds, knowing what I want, at least at this moment. With that extra bit of freedom, there has to be a tradeoff, and I secure his free arm behind his back; he won't be needing it right now. He looks up at me, a challenging expression on his face, like he's ready to duel even though it's clear that with my ammunition I'll win easily, but since that's what he ultimately wants, I guess he wins too. That kind of win/loss thinking is too confusing for me, and I shut everything else out of my mind except how this scene will end. It's the last time I'll see him, ever, so I have to make the most of it.

"I did that for a reason. Now spread those legs for me. That's good," I say soothingly, buttering him up before I take him down. I raise the crop from the desk and hold it in my hand, surveying my subject. I still don't know if he understands why I'm really angry, but this isn't about my anger anymore, it's about something much deeper and darker than that. It's sad that we won't get to play like this again, but I don't have enough time to waste on immature men who think a Top's job is to guess their fetish. I step forward so I'm again standing before him and lean down. I know he thinks I'm going to suck his cock, like I've done so many other times, but instead I go farther, licking my way along his thighs before sinking my teeth into his flesh. I bite without care for how it will feel for him, only knowing when to stop when I feel my teeth sink into tender skin and keep going.

I pause, sucking on his thigh, wondering if this will give him a hickey. I continue onto the other thigh, and feel him try to thrash against the chair.

I stand and motion to Karla to come join me. She walks towards us and presses her naked body against my back. I reach behind me and fondle her where I can, wanting to kiss her and hold her, but knowing there'll be plenty of time for that later. For now, this brief contact will have to suffice. I lead her to a chair and have her sit and observe. Then I take the crop and slide it's tip down his body, from his head down his cheek, over his chest, tapping it lightly against the clothespin for a moment before continuing. It reaches his cock and I see his arms jerk, trying to move forward to protect his precious jewels, but there's nothing he can do. I bat at him lightly, watch as his cock turns even pinker.

"Spread your legs wider," I instruct him, and he does. I raise the crop and then let loose, tapping and then hitting, harder and harder, along his inner thighs. He winces and tries to move, tries to bring his legs together but I work my knee between them, pressing gently against his balls as a reminder that I'm the one in charge. I continue this torment until I have the urge for something stronger; I only have a little room to work with between his legs. I throw the crop on the ground and straddle him, rubbing my pussy up and down along his cock. It feels good, no doubt, and for an instant I'm truly tempted to see what he would do with his cock if he could, but it's too late for that.

How many chances did he have to fuck me, and didn't? And now he wants it for some strange reason. I want to leave him tied up here but sense that he needs something more. I get out my pocket knife and swiftly slice through the bondage tape and remaining ropes. I like the way the knife feels in my hand, the implicit threat that I would never use, but he doesn't need to know that. There's so much that he doesn't need to know, will never know, now.

I push him roughly off the chair, and even though he outweighs me by a good 80 pounds, he staggers and has to catch himself to keep from falling off.

"Get up against the wall," I tell him, motioning where I want him to go. While he positions himself, I get a few more implements out of my bag, holding the firm leather of the paddle in my hand and feeling a calmness overtake me. I am about to settle a score, make us both even, give him the beating he's been secretly craving, fulfill the fantasy he's been too afraid to tell me he felt. And for that silence, ultimately, he will lose me. Ironic actually, but meant to be. I shake my head lest I stand here too much longer regretting what might have been.

"Are you ready?"

"Yes, Miss," he says quietly. He's had enough time, perhaps too much, to prepare himself. I close my eyes for a moment and focus on what I want, then open them and step over to him. If I were taller, I could simply lean forward and whisper in his ear, but suddenly I'm glad I'm not. There's no need to pretend that we share a false intimacy. This is simply a quid pro quo transaction that will give each of us something we've been craving, but also leave both of us needing more.

"I'm going to spank you with this paddle, once for every year of your age. You're going to count the strokes for me, and when I'm done you're going to stand there until we leave. Do you understand?" I allow no emotion to enter my voice.

"Yes, Miss."

I start off sharp and strong, then ease off a little, not the usual way but this is a special occasion, the first and last time for this particular configuration, and I will do it my way. After ten strokes, I pause and place my hand over his reddened skin, kneading the warmth I feel there. With each squeeze, I feel him wiggle and I press my entire body up against his. I've chosen his age for the number of whacks as a symbol of all that he should know by now and doesn't, and because I need a stopping point or we could be here forever. As I massage his ass I know that there is a part of me that will regret leaving, despite all of our differences, will regret not going farther. I wonder if it's my own fear, too, that has contributed to this détente, but even if it is, there's no going back. Before taking the next swing, I look over at the naked and sublime Karla, who is sitting and watching silently. I have no idea what she thinks, or if she understands, but I hope that she does. I keep up a solid, even pace, with well-placed blows that land just as harshly as I intended them. He tries not to make any noise but I can hear the changes in his breathing, see the way his ass moves ever so slightly as it eagerly awaits my strokes. For the last three, I turn the paddle over so the mean indentations on the other side—the one I've never dared use before—are facing him.

I step closer and say, "These last strokes are really going to hurt, so get ready." I say the words gently, tenderly, almost as if I want to protect him from myself, which in its own way is the truth. Suddenly, I want to step back, put the paddle down, leave. I don't know if I can finish the job, if I care enough to expend the energy, but I must somehow because after a deep breath, I lift my arm again.

The three of us hear the loud smack as the paddle connects with his ass, and his hand hits the wall with a thud as he tries to process the pain. I don't let that stop me, and again repeat the motion on the other cheek. Before the final blow, the room is crackling with tension; Karla is standing now, staring, rapt as I take a quick glance at her and then back at him. He is tall, big, strong, and yet vulnerable here. I feel tears prick my eyes at how much I sense that he would give me, if he knew how. I feel forgiveness settle into my body, knowing that he has not deliberately hurt me, only done the best that he could do. Alas, that was not enough for my needs, but maybe he will find someone for whom it will be.

I bring my arm back and release all of the hurt, pride, honor and forgiveness, and I almost feel it all leave me and enter him. The sound this time isn't quite as loud, but it leaves the room ringing with its noise nonetheless. I want to say something, even if it's only "goodbye," but I can't. I press my hand against his back, letting my touch do the speaking for me, before quietly gathering my things. He leans his head against the wall, his eyes closed. Before we leave, I pull Karla close to me and we hug for a long minute. Then I grab our bag and take her hand as we go. We head to the park and sit on a bench and I lean my head on her shoulder, and we sit for a long time. Maybe I was wrong. Maybe there are some things that can be said without words, with bodies and breath and movement. I lean over, bury my head in her neck and she holds me. I don't even know what I feel—relief, sadness, hope perhaps. Whatever it is, words are not enough to convey it. I smile at that, knowing that he would understand perfectly.

IN BRENDAN'S ROOM
by Lee Minxton

"So, this is the next stop on the guided tour of the ancestral Moore estate?" Angie arched an eyebrow at Brendan, who chuckled shyly.

"Such as it is, yes. My old bedroom, practically untouched since I left for college. Impressive, right?"

Angie surveyed the gleaming Chess Club trophies, the thick gray shag carpeting, and the lone Soundgarden poster on the wall. "Absolutely. And if it gives me a few minutes with you away from your wacky family, so much the better." She kissed him on the cheek, wrapping an arm around his shoulder.

Brendan rolled his eyes. "You've been great with this whole reunion thing. I mean, I don't even know who half these people are. And I can't believe you're actually wearing the dress my grandmother gave you." He took a good look at his wife. The blue floral print looked like something concocted by Laura Ashley's evil twin, but it contrasted nicely with Angie's slightly tousled dark hair and sparkling green eyes. It covered her up so completely, from shoulders to ankles, that he couldn't help thinking about the lush body hidden underneath... But there was just no way he could take advantage of the situation, what with four generations of proud repression holding court downstairs.

The frustrated teenager of the house at age 29, Brendan thought. *Some things never change.*

"It's just my little contribution to family harmony. But enjoy the dress while you can. It's ending up on the carpet in about thirty seconds."

Brendan's eyes widened behind his wire-rimmed glasses. "We couldn't." His breath caught in his throat once he noticed that his wife's free hand was caressing his balls through the placket of his trousers.

"What's stopping you?" She traced the outline of the zipper as it tormented Brendan's swelling cock.

"For one thing, the door's wide open." For the moment, it sounded like everyone was safely downstairs. But who could be sure?

Angie nudged the door shut with her foot, relishing the feel of her husband's taut balls beneath her hand. "You have no excuse now." She parted his lips with her eager tongue, feeling him responding to the deep kiss in spite of himself.

"Cocktease." Brendan was startled at the guttural sound of his voice. Half compliment, half epithet, the word seemed to come from some primal place inside him.

Angie beamed. "You know it." She pulled at his sweater, and he raised his arms involuntarily. She purred at the sight of his supple torso.

"This is crazy," he breathed as he started to work on his belt. "This room makes me feel like I'm in high school, for Chrissakes."

Angie stopped in her tracks, enunciating the phrase dreamily as Brendan kicked out of the rest of his clothes. For the first time in her life, the two words held an exotic allure. "*High school.* Mmmm. Your sister showed me your yearbook picture today. You would have driven me wild even then."

Brendan thought a second, and then cringed. He knew the photograph Angie was talking about. In it, he sported geeky glasses, a baggy flannel shirt, and a bad haircut to boot. Maybe she was mocking him...or maybe she was a bigger pervert than he had ever dreamed possible.

"You looked so adorable," she continued. "I can see it all now. Brendan Moore, the decent, studious Catholic boy. Shy around girls and a perfect gentleman on dates, but haunted by lurid fantasies as his hormones boiled hotter by the day." Angie was approaching a meltdown herself as her eyes met his. "Am I correct?"

Brendan's cheeks were crimson, his voice barely audible. "Yes."

She started to unbutton her dress, lost in reverie. "The sweetest boy in the world, all alone every night in that bed. Lying in the dark with his luscious, rockhard cock in hand, secretly wishing for someone to come give him what he craved." She heard his sharp intake of breath, and knew she was right on the money. Angie stepped out of the dress, unable to keep her voice steady. "Well, here she is. So lie back and let her take care of things."

Brendan bit his lip. All the time his bride had chatted politely with his ninety-year-old grandfather, his cousin the seminary student, and his spinster aunt, she had been wearing a demi cup bra and no underwear. Of all the nights....

She watched in satisfaction as Brendan staggered to the twin bed, not even bothering to turn down the forest-green comforter. He stretched his lanky body out slowly, and started to take his glasses off. "Leave them on," Angie chided. "I like you best that way. Glasses, but nothing else." It was true. Brendan's bespectacled face looked downright innocent, an enticing counterpoint to the already glistening cock pouting at the ceiling.

Angie unhooked her bra strap, never taking her eyes off Brendan. She shrugged the lacy fabric off, and knelt gingerly at the edge of the bed. "Let's get a good look at you, young man. Big for your age, I see." She leaned over her hapless husband, brushing her hands over his pectorals, savoring the feel of taut muscle beneath her warm palms. Brendan groaned in delight as her hands teased down his body, grazing his belly and playing with his sensitive inner thighs.

"I never had a boyfriend in high school, remember? In study hall, I used to daydream about finding some guy, sneaking into his room, and doing everything to him." She kissed Brendan hungrily, nibbling his voluptuous lower lip. "To you," she sighed, arching her back so her pert little breasts hung mere inches from his mouth. The bedspring chirped as she shifted her weight.

"I wonder how thin these walls are," he fretted. Then he took one rosy nipple in his mouth and sucked reverently. A squeal of pleasure roiled in Angie's throat as her nipple hardened between Brendan's tender lips. She ran a hand through her husband's shaggy brown hair, now darkened with sweat. She felt overwhelmed with love as she saw anxiety mingling with the lust in his hazel eyes.

"Don't worry, sweetheart. Altar boy, honor roll...they'd never suspect their dearest Brendan." She started to lick down his sternum, taking her time with him. She could feel his pulse beneath her tongue, and it excited her even more. "I know just what they'd say. 'It's that girl,'" she breathed against the muscular planes of his abdomen. "'Look what she makes our sweet boy do,'" she growled, right before she took his cock between her lips. She lapped at the viscous bead dripping down the tip, welcoming its saltiness. She teased around his silken cockhead and then began to suck eagerly. Brendan's breathing grew shallow, and his balls grew tighter in her hand.

"I'm going to *shoot* like a high school boy if you don't stop," Brendan muttered affectionately.

She released his cock, giving it one last butterfly-kiss before kneeling upright, letting her hair and breasts brush over his aching genitals as she rose. "Fair enough," she whispered, kissing him so he could taste himself. Slowly, she straddled him. Brendan winced at the ease of penetration, held captive by her cunt's snug slickness. He clutched her waist so that the full girth of him nuzzled against her.

Brendan closed his eyes, fearing that one glance at his glorious Angie would wring him dry for life. Somewhere in the distance, he could hear his mother and his great-aunt arguing over the placement of dessert forks, but it didn't matter any longer. The music of his wife's uneven breathing, coupled with his own heartbeat and the intermittent creaking of the mattress, was the only sound in the world to him. Decisively, Brendan opened his eyes and began to thrust beneath her.

She ground her hips slowly, holding back to tease him at first. His hands were everywhere at once. She was overflowing onto his balls, which were now swollen and purple like ripe plums. The lovers were delirious with pleasure, joyously heading for oblivion.

Brendan choked back a moan as the first spasm wrenched his body, jerking his head so hard that his glasses fell off. A low moan escaped Angie's lips as she shuddered in ecstasy, rejoicing in the sensation of Brendan filled her. She collapsed momentarily, then rolled off him, cherishing the vision of his spent, damp body.

"You're such a nice boy. Maybe I could come over next week...I could tutor you for finals or something."

Brendan pushed a wet tendril of hair off his wife's blushing face, kissing her tenderly. "Sounds great. Tell me, do you have a date for the prom?"

Angie laughed out loud. "I do now!"

He gazed at her in admiration, knowing how lucky he was to have found someone who'd be his true love and his libertine forever. He watched as Angie stood up and rummaged through his bureau drawer. She found an old pair of his briefs, holding them up quizzically against her pelvis. She pulled them on, stretching them over her hips. "They'll do for a couple of hours," she tossed a sly look at Brendan. "Won't they, honey?" Judging from Brendan's appreciative panting, his briefs flattered her body nicely. The couple took their time getting presentable, feeling so good that they barely flinched when someone knocked on the door.

"Hey, it's time for dinner," Brendan's sister Katie announced sternly.

"Be right there," Brendan responded. Even now, Angie was touching him all over, stifling giggles as her husband tried to modulate his voice.

Angie opened the door, all smiles in the demure flowered dress, arm in arm with her slightly dazed beloved. As they walked past Katie, Angie offered her some advice.

"Watch out for the quiet ones, dear," she confided saucily.

JANE BOND (STIRRED, NEVER SHAKEN)
by Lynne Jamneck

Sunday 07:34
It was beautiful.

No, more than that. It was simply delicious. Stunningly perfect. And I'm not describing the dire state of the jail cell I'd been sitting in for the last three and a half hours. No, the appreciation of my description belonged to something entirely different. *Someone*, rather.

Saturday 23:47
I'd been sitting at the bar, my usual corner, cozying up to a vodka tonic. As the open, raging flame of my Zippo pierced the badly lit but throbbing light inside Café Manhattan, so did the bombastic voices of:

"FBI! FBI—Freeze! Nobody Move!"

They never were an articulate bunch, the Feds. This wouldn't be the first time my Saturday evening was shot to shit by such an uncouth display of authority. And probably, it wouldn't be the last either.

Sunday 07:42
I heard her voice from down the long, cold hallway of incarceration. On a strong breath of influence, it wafted down to where I waited behind bars.

"She still not talking?" West Coast accent, I thought. Lazy, but strong. Authoritative. Just the way I liked it. Most Feds I'd encountered in the past had whiny, high-pitched tones. Not Agent O'Riley. She walked slowly down the corridor, all black suit and sleek professionalism. You could spot the Irish in her miles away. Eyes that looked right through you and left you smarting for more.

Saturday 23:52

"Alice Baker?"

That was the first time those eyes of hers ripped through me. Women and guns—they'd be the death of me yet. Instant, repressed, animal, sexual attraction. And in a cocktail bar crowded with skillfully eager women. The atmosphere was thrilling.

"You can't just come barging in here!"

Sally—the owner. Inside, I bet she was secretly squealing with delight. Now her establishment could be counted amongst the numerous cruise spots where Alice Baker had been busted. People got off on that sort of thing. The people around here, anyway.

Agent O'Riley expertly placed my hands behind my back and cuffed them.

"You're under arrest for suspicion of drug trafficking."

And like that, I was led out of the place. Hands cuffed like a common crook, wolf whistles from the back. O'Riley tried to ignore the fact that her firm hand on my arm sent shivers through us both.

Sunday 07:45

She waved the guard off before unlocking the cell door. It's a good thing they never seemed to get along, Feds and cops. Otherwise my ass would probably be inside a cell more than out on the street. Small mercies, thank god.

O'Riley could see that regular procedure wasn't going to work with me. You get a knack for understanding the looks, the body language. Maybe that's why the idiots at Narcotics called in the Feds this time. They still didn't get it. In their minds, I'd been able to get off on some unanticipated technicality every time.

A loophole in a loophole. *Boy, was O'Riley going to be pissed when I walked out of here again*, I thought.

Saturday 23:59

Curious bystanders gathered at the entrance of Manhattan. Queers weren't bothered by the presence of authorities. A hot number with a crew cut flashed me a hungry look as we exited, her eyes impressed at my persona non grata status.

"Fuck the Feds!" a voice rose from behind us.

"Keep going," O'Riley commanded from behind, her hand steering me forward. "Blue Ford, next to the curb. Get in."

She opened the back door and pushed me inside, then slid in beside me, and barked an order at the driver. I didn't catch the specifics. Too busy noticing the holstered gun underneath her jacket. Glock, metallic finish.

Sunday 08:04

"These are pretty severe charges. And you can be sure the FBI won't be as sloppy as certain other factions in your prior arrests."

"You've already been," I replied in my best cocky twang.

She frowned.

"Careless," I reiterated.

"I doubt that." She smiled boldly. Very sexy. I had a good mind to tell her the truth right then and there, but decided to toy with her some more.

Sunday 01:05

I looked straight ahead as the car took off. The driver's Q-ball head glinted underneath the overhead light. O'Riley sat close to me. I wasn't sure whether she thought I might bolt from the moving vehicle, but she obviously wasn't taking any chances. I remember thinking—hoping—that maybe she had underhanded motives.

I found it a pain that I couldn't just open my mouth and tell the truth. But once you've been caught with your paw in the proverbial cookie jar, you have to start bending to a unusual set of rules. Or cling to your pride and face the consequences. Me, I opted for the former. I'm no hero.

Sunday 08:09

"Three times you've been arrested. Three times you escaped

prison by the skin of your teeth. Fourth time's not going to be that lucky."

"Why? Because the FBI never make any mistakes? I wouldn't hang on to that belief too tightly."

"We've been watching you long enough to know just how deep your involvement in this is." O'Riley flipped through a report of some sort, raised one eyebrow. For the intent of effect, I presumed.

"Like I told the cops before," I said. "You're looking in the wrong place. Go back and start your homework over."

From the top of the corridor, one of the cops on duty yelled: "Agent O'Riley! Someone on the phone for you."

Here it comes, I thought. All that was left to do now was sit back and enjoy the show. Clearly agitated at being interrupted, she gave me a long, hard look before walking out the cell door. I was glad that things were getting to a head. Last time this happened, those snoops in ballistics stole all the bullets from my confiscated gun. No doubt they were oooh-ing and aah-ing like a bunch of morons over the clever design.

I could hear the terse, one-sided conversation Agent O'Riley was having from up the corridor, her voice raising an ever-so-infected three octaves. Smug, was I. She slammed the receiver down. Footsteps, fast and furious. Then her eyes were trying to stare me into the concrete wall. I smiled. It only served to infuriate her even further.

"Told you, didn't I?"

Her jaw muscles worked furiously. Again, it was very sexy.

"Who the hell are you?" Then a little bit more restrained: "Who do you work for?"

I pulled myself up from the rickety single bed. We were standing close to each another. I think she might have wanted to give me a good backhand across the cheek just about then. And all I could think of was what it would feel like to have her unyielding hands beneath my shirt.

"I could tell you. But I'm afraid then I'd have to kill you." I gave her my best Jane Bond smile, then left her to steam on merrily. Only because I could see revenge already culminating behind her eyes. Agent O'Riley certainly wasn't going to drop this whole shebang just yet.

Sunday 21:30

Sally welcomed me back to the bar by plying me with expensive drinks. On the house. Apparently, I'd given her the best bit of advertisement since The Straight Scene decided to run an article on gay cocktail bars being the best value for weekend leisure. Entertainment rags, always three steps behind.

I sat in my corner and waited. It didn't take long.

I recognized her perfume the moment she sat on the barstool next to me. The glint in Sally's eyes told me the rest.

She ordered a whisky, on the rocks. No surprise there. A hottie at the other end of the bar looked on in miffed disappointment as O'Riley turned to face me, blocking her view.

"Popular, aren't you?" she asked.

"Not with the Feds, that's for sure."

"You're not CIA, either."

"How do you know?"

"I have a few sources of my own."

"Kills your gut, doesn't it? Not knowing."

"I know that you've thwarted four months' worth of extensive research and planning."

"It's what I do best." I lit a cigarette and glanced past her, at the invitation at the bottom end of the bar, and smiled secretively.

"You're a tease," she said lowly, but not without provocation of her own.

"You have no idea."

"Oh I think I do."

She sipped whisky like she wanted to make love to it. I absently wondered if she was armed. Then she slapped the whiskey tumbler onto the bar counter with a resounding clink. "There's something I'd like to show you."

"Oh?"

"Is your mind always this lewdly inclined?"

"Pretty much. With the right encouragement."

She smirked. "Well?"

*****

Sunday 23:05

Her apartment surprised and impressed me. Everything was neat, clean and in its right place. Probably a Virgo, if I took the time to believe in such things. The whole lot contrasted wildly with the state of my own digs, which would probably have given her a heart attack on sight. She offered me expensive scotch, which was all she had. I didn't complain. Then she opened a filing cabinet, and with a deft flick of her fingers pulled out a rather thick file.

Aha.

"No prizes for guessing whose this is," she said, holding it up.

"I'll give credit where it's due. You have good contacts." I was glad to be carrying my gun.

"You're going to have to up the ante on the credit bit. I'm not FBI."

Fuck. Now I had to content with thoughts of sex and covering my ass. What the hell was O'Riley playing at—if that was her real name, even. Damn her. She had me by the balls, and in more ways than one. I could just kill her, I thought. Not like I hadn't had to do it before. I had license to. Would I get out the building before being cornered by nosy neighbors?

"Don't worry about killing me—you won't have to make the decision."

"What do you want?"

A sly smile formed round the corners of her pretty mouth. She tossed the file aside and strode purposefully up to where I stood; ready to pounce or run, whichever proved more viable.

"'C'mon, I know you want to. You've been dying to get your hands on me ever since I slapped cuffs on you last night. Maybe even before that."

"As true as that may be, last night you were still a lowly Fed as far as I was concerned. Now I'm not so sure."

She leaned in close, and I could feel the cold shiver of her breath on my adrenalized skin. Her hand was on my arm again, firm; déjà vu made my mind scramble.

"You don't seem like the type to run from a challenge."

How the hell had this happened? Hadn't I been the one in control up until now? That'll teach me to get over confident. Wasn't it arrogance that got me into this secret-agent-shit in the first place?

"Take off your jacket."

I raised an eyebrow in response.

"I'd like to see what I'm up against."

I tossed the denim jacket aside, revealing the black Browning Hi Power 9mm in its side holster.

"Impressive," she said. "Now, put it on the table."

"Do you think I'm nuts?"

"Maybe a little. It's part of what makes you so attractive."

"You first," I insisted.

"You're incorrigible."

"I think you've got that the wrong way around."

"Fine," she stepped even closer, making my heart skip a beat. "If it makes you feel better keep the damn thing close to you. I don't care."

And then her lips were on mine, hot and forceful and oh god...I realized then how much I wanted to fuck her. Not eloquent by any means, but the truth. The story of my life.

The heat between us made my head swim, and for more than the obvious reasons. One the one hand, my hormones were gleefully applauding. On the other, my precise sense of danger was shouting big, bold warning shots through my mind.

What are you, insane? She had you thrown in jail for chrissakes!

To make matters worse, her threat to my security made me want her even more.

Her tongue paid service to mine in the most marvelously lewd way. She licked, slowly, along the curve of my lips. I tried to keep half my mind on the experience, rationally adjusting the other half to keep a lucid eye on my gun. Her hands moved up and down my back but kept a polite distance from the weapon. She pulled away from me and our kiss ended. There was a determined look in her eye that infuriated me. At the same time I found it admirable. She'd had this planned ever since she laid eyes on me. I could tell by the subtle ways she encouraged my hands to touch her, my body to respond to hers. And Christ—it did.

My fingers pulled and worked determinedly at the edge of her tailored black slacks, looking for buttons to pop or a zip to pull.

"Are you going to tell me what's going yet?" I asked through clenched teeth. Lust turned me into a tightened coil, ready to snap.

"I'm afraid of the penalty if I do."

"Don't worry," I teased in the hollow of her neck. "I won't stop for nothing."

My fingers edged round the elastic of her knickers; at the same time I felt her hands grope at the clasp of my holster-sling.

"Yes, for godsakes, take it off," I sneered into her neck. The weapon fell to the floor with a resounding thump. She took my free hand and roughly shoved it underneath her crisp, collared shirt. Barely had I unhooked her bra and thrown it on the floor when she pulled my T-shirt over my head. She seemed pleased at the sensibleness of my underwear which contrasted with the frilly slip of a thing she'd still been wearing moments before.

She pulled me to against her, our naked skin separated only by my hand which couldn't seem to undo itself from her perfectly fashioned breasts. Her nipples responded in kind, straining into hard, stiff points as my fingertips teased and pinched them.

My other hand had finally breached the outer limits of her underwear. She fought against me—whether for real or because she knew that it would turn me on I'm not sure. Her breath chased in sexy, wanting gasps as my fingertips quietly stroked her clit into hard compliance. I remembered how cocky she had been the night before. Dragging me out of that bar like some punk—just a regular thug. How confident she'd been then. How *in control*. It drove my butch sensibilities weak with lust to now have her in such a compromising position.

I heard her say: "Kiss me."

She was still every bit as demanding, though. "Please?" I needled.

"Fuck you."

"You *are* confused," I replied. "But I forgive you, given the circumstance." With one smooth shove I managed to back her up against a sturdy-looking bookcase. A quick glance showed it lined with an assortment of crime and psychology volumes. This amused me to some extent. I hoped she didn't think that she had me all figured out.

Then I gave in and kissed her anyway, simply because I wouldn't deny myself the bliss of her lips.

There was a sexy little sigh from her throat, and then her mouth opened silently beneath mine as I entered her. Some of her books tumbled from their perch onto the floor. Footsteps sounded close-by as neighboring occupants traveled past the front door, conversing loudly.

"Sshhh " I mouthed while effectively working her beautiful body into the wood-finish. Her hands reached into my hair and pulled me closer, making even more books tumble to the ground. She pushed my head down, my mouth to her strenuously erect nipples.

I made a mental note as to how far exactly my gun was, and then took one nipple between my lips and sucked, languidly. One of her legs hooked round my hip, pulling me closer. The thin, warm film of sweat on the inside of her thigh brushed against my hand as she tried to get me deeper into her. She pulled my head up. Her tongue was in my mouth again, trying to keep herself quiet while the voices on the other side of the door took their sweet fucking time to move on. I felt the inevitable tightening of her cunt around my wet fingers, her hands pulling at my hair and raking along the naked skin of my back. By then I couldn't give a continental shit if anyone heard us (for all I knew it might be my last great deed before she killed me, the praying mantis bitch). My sexual instincts went into overdrive. I fucked her so devotedly that something much heavier than a book toppled to the floor with a hammering thud. I didn't worry to look. Her back arched, hips pushing into mine and she exhaled into my throat, knocking wind straight into my lungs.

Well.

At least the noise in the hallway had found sudden silence.

Monday 7:59

I felt a little blind, the way I darted out of her apartment. I left O'Riley in a comfortable daze on her three-seater couch, grabbed my gun and hijacked out of there.

I didn't think that she'd still try and kill me after that, but in my line of business you can never be too sure. Besides, I had to get a fresh start. Monday was my official report to the boss day, and if I didn't show up on time, there would be hell to pay. The man did me a favor by rescuing me from twenty years in prison. The CIA was still pissed at him for jumping the gun on them and getting to me first.

"Baker," he growled as I strode into his office. He had an unusual smirk on his pockmarked face. He leaned back in his chair, hands folded. "I'm impressed. You passed the test brilliantly."

"What test?"

He pressed a button on his telephone and spoke into the speakerphone:

"Send her in."

"What's going on?"

"We had a little test to confirm your loyalty to The Agency."

I had a sudden sinking feeling in my stomach. The thick double doors to his office opened. There stood O'Riley. Smiling at me like a cat who just had a saucer of cream.

"I believe you've met Agent Six. One of our premier crime psychologists with the Washington crew. Don't worry. She passed you with flying colors."

KINSEY SIX
by Thomas S. Roche

When I get home, I almost turn around and walk out. I can hear you moaning. It's almost two in the morning; you said it was fine if I came home by midnight, so I'm pissed. The bedroom door is wide open. I can hear the two of you moaning, and I've got a straight line of sight into the bed, where you're spread open and she's between your thighs.

We discussed this. We decided it was important to you to keep this partner, to remain lovers with her even though you and I had made a commitment. It's called poly-fucking-amory, and the most important thing about it is that we keep our agreements, isn't it? The fact that I've come home two hours after you said it was okay, and you're still fucking like bunnies with the bedroom door open, makes a surge of rage go through me.

But I watch. I don't turn around and walk out, because it's so damn late and I don't want to go get a motel or kill time at the 24-hour diner.

And besides, I've never seen Cora naked before.

She's sprawled out on the bed, hanging over the edge as she eats you out. Her nude body is slender, even skinny, but her hips have just enough swell to make my eyes linger there. She's got a tattoo of two female symbols intertwined on her lush ass. Her legs are spread and I can see her pussy, shaved and pierced.

Your eyes open and you see me in the doorway. You smile.

Shameless. You're fucking looking at me and not even caring that you've broken your agreement with me, that you and Cora are still fucking when I walk in the door. But you don't stop, you don't ask Cora to stop. Instead, you blow me a kiss.

Then Cora lifts her head from your pussy and turns to look over her shoulder, her face glistening in the flicker of candlelight. You always light candles when you fuck.

Cora smiles.

"Hi, Mike," she says, and winks at me.

Then she goes back to eating your pussy.

Watching you, I feel my cock stirring in my pants. You've locked eyes with me and I can't look away. Your lips part and you start moaning again as Cora returns to tonguing your clit. You've described that technique to me many times, told me how she does it, but I've never quite been able to get it perfect. Cora has got it perfect. I can tell you're going to come.

I think back on the conversation we had where we negotiated this. "We'll be done by midnight, and she'll sleep on the couch," you said. "I promise, you won't have to see anything."

"It's all right if you're not done by midnight," I assured you. "Just make sure you close the bedroom door."

You smiled, kissed me on the forehead. "Oh, we'll close the bedroom door," you told me. Then, with a wicked smile, you added, "Unless we want you to join in."

At the time, I'd blown it off, thinking from the girlish giggle you gave that you were just teasing me. After all, Cora's a lesbian, isn't she? A dyed-in-the-wool femme Kinsey 6, you told me. I ignored it.

But after all, a deal is a deal.

We should negotiate this, shouldn't we? Fuck it. The die is cast.

I take my clothes off. You watch me as I do, never offering a protest, just moaning in time with Cora's tongue on your clit. Cora doesn't even look up until I'm already naked, until my cock is standing out straight and hard and I'm next to the bed, watching from an improved vantage point as her face works up and down between your thighs. That's when she looks up at me and smiles.

"Oooh," she said. "I thought you'd never ask."

She reaches up and grabs my cock, pulling me down onto the bed. Her mouth, the mouth that's moved so skillfully on your clit, closes over my cock and she swallows it down, her lips working up and down on my shaft as I look down into her pretty face. She's got her eyes upturned toward me, and in the candlelight I can see the shimmer inside them. You lean forward and wrap your fingers around the base of my cock, feeling Cora's lips linger halfway down my shaft.

"Cora hasn't sucked cock in ten years," you say. "Don't you feel honored?"

"Hell, yes," I say, as your face burrows under Cora's and you begin to kiss my balls. I kneel there on the bed not knowing what to do, but Cora's sprawled out under me with her gorgeous ass looking delectable, and her legs are spread wide. I'm enough taller than her that I can lean over and reach between them.

When I touch her pussy I feel how incredibly wet she is. Her whole body stiffens, and for a moment I think I've gone too far. Then she moans rapturously, the vibrations traveling through my hard cock and into my body, and she starts to suck my cock in earnest as I finger her pussy.

You kneel on the bed and kiss me, your tongue lazing into my mouth as you run your fingers through my hair. "She wants you to fuck her," you whisper. "She's been talking about it all night."

"I thought she was a Kinsey 6," I hiss.

"Haven't you heard?" you whisper. "There's a new scale. She's right in the middle."

Then you lean down close to her and say, "Mike's going to fuck you now, Cora."

You guide me around behind her, and I slide easily between her spread thighs. The rings of her lips prickle my shaft as I slide into her. She gasps, her pussy tight as it embraces me. You position yourself at her face, spreading your legs so she can eat you as I fuck her from behind. Her hand goes underneath her and she starts to work her own clit. I fuck her slowly at first, picking up speed as she begs, "Harder, Mike, harder!" her fingers moving faster on her clit as she urges me on. Then I feel her pussy clenching around my shaft as she moans into your cunt, and that's all it takes to send me over the edge. As she finishes coming, I let myself go inside her, filling her with my come.

The three of us crawl up on the bed, and Cora and I start kissing while you cuddle up next to us and watch, lazily stroking your cunt. I can taste your pussy on her mouth.

"I guess you're not a six any more," I say.

"Let's call it five point five," she whispers, and curves her fingers around my soft cock, slick with her juices. You kiss my ear, your tongue warm.

LUST BE A LADY
by Michelle Houston

What most people don't realize when they go to a strip club is that the girls are not there for the customers. The customers are there for the girls. The strippers aren't meat, up on stage merely to be ogled. They make a conscious decision to be there, and to make as much money off of each customer as they can.

For some people, a nudie magazine is enough to get them hot and bothered. For other folks, a few passionate sentences strung together will take them to the edge. Some get off on the sting of the whip, or the thrill of being in control, or the thought of almost getting caught, or one of any number of other fetishes.

For Amber, it was the feel of skin and money against her body. Nothing turned her on like a calloused hand sliding up her inner thigh, trailing a one-dollar bill. She thrived on being a stripper, and it showed. The slick feel of sweaty skin on skin was a turn on, and adding money into the equation only made it that much better.

Tall as an Amazon, with her science-enhanced breasts and the luck-of-thegenetics-draw body and face, she could have easily gotten a job modeling. But she preferred black lights to the spotlight.

As the DJ called out her name, she shimmied onto the stage to a whispery beat. Slow and sensuous, she danced for the audience, paying attention to who was reaching for a wallet and who wasn't.

Gripping the poll, she swung herself up, spinning—dress flaring around her. With a perfectly planned routine in mind, she already knew what she was going to do and when. Stripping was an art form to her, and she a patient artist. The stage wasn't going to get her what she wanted. Later, in the private rooms, she received her pay-off. There, almost anything was allowed, provided the customer was willing to pay for it.

But she had to tease the customers into requesting a private dance. She had to make them want her; make them think they might actually get her. The menwere the easiest, but the women—*they* were the thrill.

As she moved around the stage, thrusting her hips while undoing buttons on her peek-a-boo lace dress, she caught the eye of a petite blonde and smiled. Tentatively, the blonde smiled back. Across the stand, Amber danced, moving closer and closer to her target.

At every outstretched hand, she paused and squatted, displaying her smooth shaven pussy for her cool bill. Some pressed a dollar into her garter—those who were more daring stopped her longer, slipping in a second dollar. For the extra bill, she made sure to clench her ass, causing her pussy to quiver.

As she stood again, she tossed her gown aside, baring her sweat-glistening flesh. Several gasps filled the air as her slender yet supple body was finally seen.

After several moments, she reached the blonde and crouched low. Clenching her legs tight, she dropped back onto her hands, arching her back. Some would call her pose obscene, but Amber knew this was what her customers craved most—her pussy shoved right into their face. Within reach, but still forbidden.

As the blonde slipped a dollar into her garter, Amber twisted, pulling her upper body forward, and shifted her hips. Back into her standard pose, she leaned forward, barely brushing her breasts against the blonde's face. Pulling back, she caught the customer's gaze.

Hooked.

Slightly glazed, the petite woman watched Amber as she moved back and stood. Slowly bending over, Amber offered a new view of her pussy as around her, hands lifted more dollars, slipping them into her garter belt. Smiling at the blonde, she straightened and strutted away.

While she continued her onstage tease, she kept an eye on the blonde. Amber knew she had her; the woman clearly liked what she saw. But was she willing to pay to see more?

The final beat of her second song filled the room, and Amber stopped midstride. Turning to look over her shoulder, she caught the blonde's eye and winked. After bending down and showing off one more time, she grabbed her gown and left the stage. The next girl was called up, and the tease began again.

A towel was pressed into her hand, and Amber took a few moments to dry her damp skin and freshen up. She unlocked her locker and slipped her tips inside her purse, then made sure to lock it securely again.

Selecting a new outfit, this time a skimpy plaid pleated skirt and a white button-up shirt, she made certain each piece was easy to remove, yet flattered her to perfection. While the men tended to want slutty, she had found from experience that most women preferred a tasteful tease.

As she stepped out into the room from a side door, she paused to scan the room; both for the blonde and for any other interested eyes turned her way. Seeing several men eyeing her, she knew that tonight was going to be one of her good nights.

With a slow, confident stride, she started into the room, stopping to chat with the most interested-looking guys. She promised several lap dances later, to some disappointment, but Amber made sure the guys were smiling before she moved on.

It was a delicate line she walked—turning down sure things for a possibility. But more often than not, it was well worth it.

She headed straight for her slim target, then licked her lips when she caught the blonde's eye. Amber could tell that the woman was nervous, anxious, yet willing. They always were. It just took an extra bit of teasing to loosen them up.

With a flick of her hair over her shoulder, Amber stopped right at the blonde's table.

"This seat taken?" she drawled, sex lacing every word. As she waited, she twisted her hair into a knot. Her raised arms strained her breasts against her tight, half-buttoned shirt.

"Um, no."

Settling herself carefully in her chair, Amber made sure her position was comfortable, but still showed off her assets. Holding out her hand, Amber introduced herself.

A slender hand met hers, trembling within her grasp. "I'm Shannon."

"Nice to meet you, Shannon. Your first time?"

"Yes."

Pulling away, Amber settled back into her chair and shifted again, moving closer. Lifting up a cigarette from the pack on the table, she motioned to the lighter.

"May I?"

"Sure. Yeah. Go ahead."

Amber set the cigarette between her lips and waited, her gaze locked on Shannon's. After a moment, the blonde's eye widened as she caught the hint. Reaching across the table, the picked up the lighter and struck the flint. A small flame leapt from the top and she leaned even closer—lighting Amber's cigarette. Her mouth a perfect O, Amber exhaled, then licked her ruby lips.

As Shannon leaned back, Amber dropped a hand under the table. With one hand she smoked, with the other she traced tiny circles on her own inner thighs.

"So I'm sure you're curious about how all of this works, right?" Shannon nodded quickly.

"Basically, you can tip the girls on stage. That's the first step. After that are the dances. Twenty for a table dance—" she took in Shannon's blank stare, and then continued to explain, "that's where the girls dances for you out here, in front of everyone." Amber paused to take drag off of her cigarette before reciting the rest of the charges. "Thirty for a private dance. You go into a small room in the back with the dancer, and she can actually touch you as she dances, but you can't touch her. For forty and up, depending on what you want, you can get a little light touch, and a lot of grinding. That's what gets a lot of the guys go for. Now for the female customers, we have a special offer, a dildo dance."

Amber paused again, stubbing her cigarette out in the ashtray.

"That's fifty dollars. You get a lap dance, and during that, you can masturbate. We have a sex shop in the lobby where you can purchase a toy before you dance if you want." Looking up, she met her customer's interested gaze. "So tell me, Shannon, what interests you?"

Beneath the table, Amber moved her hand from her thigh to Shannon's knee and waited, her thumb stroking slowly across bare skin.

"Do you want a lap dance, honey?" Amber asked softly. "Do you want me to tease you, out here with everyone watching? With guys fantasizing about us together? Or do you want to go somewhere private."

"Um, private. I like the idea of being watched, but not here."

"Okay, sweetheart. Then let's go." Standing, Amber reached for Shannon's hand and helped her out of the chair, then guided her across the room.

Several guys hooted and whistled as they made their way past the tables, around the bar and into a hallway of doors. At an open door, Amber stepped inside, pulling Shannon with her. As the door closed with a faint click, Shannon jumped. Nervously, she licked her lips. "So, do I give you the money now? Or after?"

Amber settled herself onto the leather couch and patted the cushion next to her. "Just come over here and sit down for a minute."

As Shannon settled next to her, Amber placed a hand on her thigh and then trailed her fingers up and down the smooth skin, from knee to skirt hem. "This is for you, honey. Before, after, during, whatever makes you most comfortable. If anything I do excites you, tell me so I can do more of it. And if anything I do makes you uncomfortable, tell me and I'll stop."

One handed, Amber unclasped her hair from the twisted knot at the back of her head and let it flow freely. Her other hand continued its path up and down Shannon's thigh. "So what do you want, Shannon? You want a dance? Or do you want to climax while I dance for you?"

"I want to—" the blonde hesitated. "I want to come."

"Mmmm, that can be arranged. Lift your hips and let's get this skirt off of you, so you can get to your pussy." Moving her hands to Shannon's hips, Amber pulled the skirt down her thighs, then let the soft fabric pool at her feet. "Much better."

Amber carefully stood and moved directly in front of the petite blonde and nudged Shannon's thighs apart. Lifting her hands to her blouse, Amber started to dance. Slowly, she shifted from side to side, her movements subtle. She wasn't dancing as much as she was seducing, every movement intended to arouse her partner further.

Shannon's gaze stayed glued to Amber's hands as the dancer caressed her own body. As Amber's shirt came off, baring her pert breasts, with pebble hard nipples, Shannon gasped and slid one hand into her panties, touching herself. Leaning down, Amber brushed her nipples against her customer's cheeks, then her lips, teasing with a brush of skin against skin, before pulling away.

Her hands on the knot of her skirt, Amber untied it, her hips swaying. As it floated around her, a plaid waterfall, Amber kneeled on the couch. Straddling Shannon, she started to arch against her. Amber's breasts brushed against Shannon's silk shirt, and then she lifted her hands to the woman's shoulders and massaged her slender neck.

"Relax baby," she whispered. "Just let the music move you." Grinding her hips downward, she pressed her bare pussy against Shannon's knee. Whimpering slightly, Amber arched back, then ground down again. It was a fine line she walked, between dancing and fucking.

Brushing her breasts against Shannon's lips again, she let the blonde lightly kiss them, before pulling back. Each shift away was harder than the last, but it was worth it. Shannon's eyes glazed slightly, her breath coming in harsh gasps.

"That's it baby. Relax. Just feel the music."

Beneath her panties, Shannon's hands were going wild. Her knuckles were arched, brushing against Amber's pussy through the thin silky fabric, teasing Amber into a frenzy of motion. The dancer could feel her own orgasm building as her customer crested, lost in the sensations.

Drawing back at the last moment, Amber denied herself that which her pussy ached for. Collapsing on the couch next to Shannon, she moved her hands once again over her own body, teasing herself, but still denying.

Her eyes closed, Shannon shifted against her, setting her face against Amber's bare breast. For a few moments, Amber held the woman close, stroking her hands through Shannon's hair as her breathing calmed.

"Mmmm," Shannon murmured as she pulled away. A faint blush stained her cheeks. "Thank you," she whispered as she stood and pulled her skirt up. Amber sat there and watched her, a tender smile on her face.

"It was my pleasure, honey."

Her clothing mostly in order, Shannon reached into her pocket and pulled out a fifty-dollar bill. "Can I ask for you when I come back?"

"Of course."

Accepting the money, Amber leaned back against the couch and watched Shannon leave. Desire still humming her veins, she reached under the couch and pulled out a small black bag. Setting the fifty aside, she unzipped the bag and pulled out her vibrator and a dollar bill.

Thighs spread, she thrust the vibrator into her dripping pussy, closed her eyes and started to rub the crisp bill over her sweat-dampened flesh.

MORE
by Michele Zipp

Another Monday morning.

The white grains of sugar fell from the spoon into a yellow mug of black coffee. Mary stared at the counter through the stray strands of red hair that fell from her ponytail, but it was the aroma of the Colombian ground that made her blink. As she poured in the milk and stirred, Scott came up behind her, kissing her on her neck while wrapping his warm, freshly showered hands around her waist. His wet blond hair left a trickle of water on her cheek.

"I'm running late, sweetie. No coffee for me today," he said as he turned to walk into their bedroom to get dressed. "Do you know where my brown briefcase is?" he called from the other room.

"In the hall closet, behind the old laundry basket."

"Found it."

After giving Mary another kiss, Scott rushed out the door. Mary settled into the couch with her coffee and laptop. Although the caffeine was already working through her system, she didn't feel any creative energy. She was in a rut and she knew it. The deadline for her latest writing assignment was in seven days, but she had no inspiration. Whenever she tried to write, she came up lacking. Her writing rut mirrored the rut she was in with Scott. They loved each other dearly, but they barely had sex anymore—somewhere along the course of their relationship, they'd lost their spark.

She wasn't sure what it was that they needed. Something. Everything. More.

Staring at the blank computer screen, Mary took another sip of her coffee and stretched her legs to the floor. She still had on her thin white T-shirt and pale pink pajama sweats, and she felt a shiver rush through her, despite the warmth of the coffee. To thwart the chill in their apartment, she headed into the bedroom to put on a sweater. On the dresser sat Scott's black briefcase. It was open and amongst the scattered pieces of paper was a black postcard with a picture of an old keyhole. Under the keyhole read "You're invited." Mary turned the glossy card over and saw an image of silhouetted bodies in the throes of lust. Below was a phone number written in bright red ink.

Mary brought the card back to the sofa. Although she tried to work, she found herself drawn repeatedly to the shiny black card. What was it for and why did Scott have it? After several rounds of trying to push the thoughts from her head, she took the card to the kitchen phone and dialed the number.

A sweet sounding woman answered. "Name?" the female voice asked.

"Mary," she replied.

"Mary. What is you last initial?"

"A."

"What is the password, Mary A.?"

Mary quickly hung up. *Password?* Why did she need a password? A password to what?

She waited twenty minutes until she knew that Scott would be at his desk. Then she called. "Where did you get this invitation?" Mary immediately asked.

"Hello to you, too," Scott teased.

"Where did you get it?" She wasn't letting up.

"Jimmy gave it to me. The invitation is for one of those kinky kinds of parties you hear about sometime. I thought that maybe we could go check it out."

There was silence on Mary's end.

"The password is 'ignition,'" he shared.

"Ignition, huh? When is it?"

"This Friday night," he said. "What do you think?"

Mary hesitated. This had always been one of her naughtiest

desires. Being on display for other people, engaging with strangers in a sexy menage a something. But could she actually go through with it?

"I'll leave it to you to RSVP if you want to go," Scott said into her silence.

She wrote down the password on the flyer so she wouldn't forget it while she tried to make her decision. Ignition. She knew that Scott wouldn't push her, wouldn't force her to do something she didn't want to. But that wasn't the problem—she *did* want to. Ignition. She stared at the word for awhile, then placed the postcard in her purse. Conflicted, she sat in front of the TV with her laptop on her lap and the remote control in her hand.

Over lunch on Wednesday at Le Caf* with Scott, Mary pulled out the postcard. "Should we call now?" she asked him, a lilt in her voice. She hadn't been able to stop thinking about the sex party for the past two days.

"I dare you," he urged.

Without giving it a second thought, Mary dialed the number.

"Name?" the female voice asked.

"Mary," she replied.

"Mary. What is you last initial?"

"A."

"What is the password, Mary A.?"

"Ignition."

"See you Friday. Location: 1244 Ninth Street."

With the cell phone still pressed against her ear, Mary smiled while Scott waited in anticipation to find out what had been said on the other end of the phone.

"Grab a pen and write this down," she instructed. "1244 Ninth Street. I guess we *are* going," she said with a devious grin, and he leaned across the table and kissed her. It was a different kind of kiss than they'd shared for a long time. A kiss that made her think maybe the end of their rut was in sight.

Louise was a leggy, thin brunette who worked as a therapist at City Hospital. She was dating Julian, an artist and incurable romantic with hazel eyes guaranteed to make Louise melt any time he looked at her. She grazed her pale pink fingertipped hands through his light brown hair while they were waiting for a table at Le Caf*. Scott and Mary had just left and a table was free. Positioned between the salt and pepper shaker were two menus and the black postcard that the couple had left behind.

"I think I'm going to get a cheeseburger," Julian said. "What about you?"

"Ignition," she said with a hint of curiosity in her voice.

Confused, Julian tipped his menu down to see what Louise was talking about. There in her hand was the glossy black card with the word "ignition" written next to the phone number.

"Wonder what that's about," Julian said while looking at the peep hole graphic on the card.

Louise took out her cell phone and dialed the number. She was an adventurous girl, always up for something new.

"Name?" the female voice asked.

"Louise," she replied.

"Louise. What is you last initial?"

"D."

"What is the password, Louise D.?"

Louise hesitated. She looked at Mary's handwritten scrawl. "Ignition."

"See you Friday. Location: 1244 Ninth Street."

Reaching into her purse, Louise grabbed a pen and wrote down the address on the card. Looking at Julian, she replied to his question, "We'll find out Friday."

Clad in an open-back, little black dress, Mary fastened her long hair in a low ponytail. Her long, red tresses adorned the pale while skin of her back. It was Friday. She'd never dressed for a sex party before. She hoped her attire was appropriate.

Scott had on wearing an all black designer suit. His silver tie was draped around his black shirt. Without speaking, he walked up to Mary and she began to tie his tie. "We won't do anything without getting approval from each other. And when one of us wants to leave, we just have to say the word," Scott said.

Over the last two nights, they had gone through several steamy scenarios of what might happen at this Ignition Party, and the idea alone had made their sex life hotter than it had been in months. Mary was more vocal in bed about what she wanted and what she needed for Scott to pleasure her, and Scott's dirty talk made Mary's imagination go wild. For the first time in their relationship, Mary and Scott were ready to experiment—ready to live out their wildest fantasies.

When they made a left onto Ninth Street, Scott looked directly at Mary. "Are you ready for this?" She smiled and kissed him hard on the lips. "Oh, yes." She was more than ready. Ignition was the password, and she was on fire.

They cleared their name on the guest list and were allowed through the door and into a different world. Inside, there was a long red carpeted hallway. The lights from above were soft, accenting the red and gold painted walls. Sounds of soft, jazzy music came from the rooms, which lined both sides of the hall. The doors to the rooms were doublewide and each was draped with a sheer piece of fabric slightly obscuring the view inside. The curtains were white, red, and black and each softly billowed in and out of the rooms from the air inside them. Mary found the scent in the hall intoxicating—a mix of jasmine and musk that tickled her senses.

"Shall we?" Scott asked, taking her hand.

Mary nodded, nervous energy giving way to deep curiosity, and let him lead her down the hall. She and Scott passed a white-curtained entrance first. Lit only by candles and various sticks of incense, the room had five bodies writhing together on a king-sized white pillow set against a white shag rug. A long-haired man's tongue and hands explored a short-haired woman's breasts; while another man explored the woman's folds as she arched her back and moved her hips to feel him in all the right spots. Another man and woman lay next to the threesome. Mary and Scott watched as the man's hands massaged the woman's thighs. He moved them down to her feet, and she let out a gasp of pleasure. Moving his hands up again, the man lingered long on her innermost thighs, putting the pressure on her clit with his fingers. She looked to be in ecstasy.

As she stared mesmerized at the bodies on the bed, Mary could feel a surge of heat between her own thighs. Scott took his hand and ran it down her ponytail, and along her exposed back, stopping just short of her ass. He left his hand on the small of her back as she silently begged it to go lower. She felt another hand on the side of her face and a soft pair of wet lips started to kiss her neck. As she turned, she was almost lost in the thick locks of a brunette. The woman was licking her way down Mary's neck. It was Louise. Scott's hand remained on Mary's back, but his mouth was now kissing the other side of her neck. Julian walked to the next doorway, where the red curtain seemed to invite him in.

Louise took Mary's hand in hers and attempted to lead her toward Julian. Mary looked back at Scott, who smiled and held her other hand. The trio followed Julian together.

Elaborate red lamps filled the red-curtained room. Giant, red velvet pillows covered the floor and three plush burgundy couches aligned the walls. The overhead fans stirred the air and Louise's long locks were tousled with the manufactured wind. an attractive young couple sprawled on one of the couches. The woman wore only a black tank top and sat astride of her man, upright and kissing him as his hands gripped her ass. Louise walked up to the couple and lifted the black tank top off the woman, then removed her own shirt. The man reached up toward Louise to fondle her perfectly rounded breasts.

Sensing her nervousness, Scott took Mary and lay her down on the pillows.

"I want you to live out your fantasy," he whispered in her ear. "I want to taste you, Mary, and fuck you while these strangers get turned on by hearing you moan with pleasure."

She turned toward him and kissed him passionately. And with her hands on his shoulders, she pushed him down toward her pussy. He trailed his way down to her thighs, lifting her dress up to reveal her lacy black G-string. Scott pulled her panties to one side. His tongue was like velvet, moving fast then slow at all the right moments. Her pleasure was intense, but she knew this was just the beginning. Above her, she could see Julian who now joined Louise and the couple. Julian's nude six-foot frame stood next to the couch as Louise knelt over the side to pleasure him with her mouth. The woman had pulled down Louise's skirt and was stroking her long legs as her man lay under her giving her pleasure with his mouth.

Mary lost herself in the sensations that Scott was giving her and her eyes were closed, but soon she felt more hands start to roam her skin. As she opened her eyes, she saw Louise moving in close to her face. The two women began to kiss and the smooth texture of Louise's lips made Mary's pussy pulse with even more anticipation. Scott stayed between Mary's legs when Louise pulled off her little black dress, exposing Mary's hard nipples. Louise's soft lips moved to Mary's nipples and she slowly circled her tongue over each one. Trembling, Mary reached out and tangled her hands in Louise's hair. She moved her hands down, feeling the curve of the pretty woman's neck and the softness of her breasts. She could feel Louise's hand join Scott's tongue on her throbbing clit. Mary was eager to come, but both her lovers sensed when she was about to explode and slowed down just to build the intensity even more.

Scott and Louise moved together on Mary's wet cunt. Her legs were spread as far as they could and her hands gently pulled at Louise's hair, which decorated her chest. She felt paralyzed with pleasure. Suddenly, there were in her own hair and when she looked up, she saw Julian. He knelt down over her and allowed the tip of his cock to touch her lips.

Oh, god, she thought. *Could she do this? Was she ready—*

She pushed her tongue out to circle the head and then released her hands from Louise's hair to tease Julian some more. He tasted sweet as she traced his shaft with the tip of her tongue, softly squeezing the head of his cock with her hand. Julian took one hand and gripped the base of his cock hard and let out a soft moan. She could feel Scott's hot breath leave her pussy and then only Louise's tongue was licking her clit. Scott's repositioned himself so that he could enter her as Louise grazed her tongue up his hard shaft. Louise straddled Mary's body facing Scott, and with her hands guided him into her.

It was an intensity of pleasure that Mary had never felt before. The anticipation of what part of her body was going to be stimulated next made every inch of her flesh even more excitable. With her eyes closed, she felt Julian's finger in her mouth and his hot lips sucking on her neck. Louise's thighs wrapped around her own, and Scott's hard cock filled her as he lifted her ass to take all of him. As Mary's orgasm reached its height, Scott found his peak and together they collapsed in ecstasy. Louise and Julian lay beside Mary and stroked her long red hair.

The red light in the room seemed to add heat to their foursome. Mary shuddered as she gazed at her three lovers, and then she smiled at Scott and said one single word: "More."

Mary woke in her own bed. Scott was snuggled up behind her, her cheek resting on his arm. Her body was still tingling. She reached back and ran her hand through Scott's hair and he reciprocated by snuggling even closer. She could feel his cock, hard against her ass.

Last night was all the inspiration she needed.

NEVER MISS YOUR WATER
by Charlie Anders

My apartment looked like a small town after a flood. I remembered flooding in South Carolina from childhood: the world had done a strip tease as the waters had receded, showing familiar items gone and others thrown out of context. Leah's friends had carted off the teak furniture and Art Nouveau decorations, leaving my stuff—paperbacks, boxes of comics, a shaggy recliner—naked in space.

And then there was the water. For the umpteenth time, I tried the kitchen tap. Again, the pipes grunted but nothing came out. I gave a thirsty growl.

Then I heard honking followed by shouts. "Hey, Rich! Get your ass down here!" I ran to the window and stuck my head out to see a Jeep crammed with bottles. Big blue bottles, the kind they put on the water coolers in offices. On the sidewalk, my friend Maria squatted with her arms around a bottle, grunting theatrically. For a moment, I just stared in disbelief. "You gonna help me or what?"

"Coming!" I ran out and down the stairs. Maria met me at the front door and hugged me. Her brown ponytail smacked my face and her Laura Ashley skirt rustled against my legs—two reminders how the butch nerd I'd known in college had changed. I felt her hand linger on the back of my neck. My skin woke at her touch. "God, I can't tell you how grateful I am. This was kind of the last thing I needed on top of everything."

"Don't mention it. It just involved dragging these monsters out of the office without my boss or coworkers noticing, then loading them into my Jeep at the cost of several lumbar vertebrae. I could only nab half a dozen. Hope that's OK."

"That's plenty. You deserve a backrub."

Maria's eyes twinkled at the offer. Even though Maria or I could have lifted the jugs by ourselves, it was way easier with two of us. She grabbed the spout and I backed up the stairs, opening the building's door with the base of the bottle wedged against my chest. Our hands kept brushing as we negotiated the dingy stairwell's corners.

"So when are they turning it back on?"

"I'm not sure. They may take a few days, but they also have some penalties and fees that I'll have to scrounge." Maria wondered aloud which one of us had ignored the bill so long, so just to be petty I showed her the chore chart in the kitchen, with "water bill" next to my ex-wife's name.

I felt Maria's breath on my neck as I bent over to phalanx the bottles on my kitchen floor. I told myself I was imagining things; we'd been friends forever. Then we stood looking across the kitchen at each other. She smiled at me, one arm draped across a burner. "I'm sorry." I indicated my sweaty body. "I didn't get a shower this morning, for obvious reasons."

"You look like someone—" Maria paused to pop the thick top off one of the jugs— "who could use a hot bath."

My biggest pan, a crockpot, holds a gallon or two. We had lots of time to talk in the kitchen while it boiled. I felt as if I should be talking about the breakup, but I couldn't get any words out. So we mostly watched the crockpot until it boiled. Then Maria grabbed it with my frayed potholders, and marched into the bathroom. Steaming water sloshed the enamel and left the tub maybe one finger full. Onto that, Maria added cold water from the bottle. "This requires a lot of sponging to work," she said. "We can add more hot water in a few minutes."

"Thanks." I hugged her. We took the pot back to the kitchen and started more water boiling. "So I guess you should be going."

"And let you boil yourself like a lobster? This is a two-person operation, and you need an engineer like me. Too bad my apartment's so far, or I'd let you shower there." It did sound plausible, and Maria had always been the pragmatic one. Even so, I took off my clothes slowly while Maria waited, arms folded. She'd never seen me naked—in years, nobody had but Leah and a few guys at the Y. I clambered into the tub and felt my balls tug upwards in the warm water. Floral bath-oil odors came as the water released the tub's memories of more opulent times. The base of my spine sighed as the water lapped at it.

Maria rolled up her sleeves and produced a loofah she'd found in a cabinet. I heard sloshing, then little teeth gnawed my vertebrae. Warm water cascaded down my back, making me shiver as the rest of me realized how cold it was. More sloshing, then the teeth returned, a little softer this time. "You've got to relax," Maria said. I felt her arm reach around, then the teeth were at my nipples. I gasped. Warmth pooled in the indentation above my gut.

"Damn." Maria stopped sponging. "These sleeves keep coming unrolled. Wait a sec." I opened my eyes—when exactly had I closed them?—to see her unbuttoning her blouse. It slid off revealing a bra with birds on it. Then she slid off her skirt. The panties and bra matched.

"Maria, I'm not ready for another relationship —"

"This isn't a relationship. This is a bath."

I could never fault Maria's logic.

She nudged me gently until I lay backwards, arms behind my head and knees steepled. She slid the loofah up my side, warming my ribs and trickling water along my chest. She ended in my left armpit. I squirmed as the sponge rutted amongst the hair. "Hold still. Actually, I think the water's boiling again."

I fell asleep in the shallow lukewarm water, the loofah perched on my sternum.

A geyser woke me. A hot flood engulfed my balls. "This is why you need an engineer. Bet that feels good, huh?" I opened my eyes. Maria had the crockpot at an incline on the side of the tub and was pouring so that no boiling water actually touched my skin, but it hit the water at just the right point to lick between my legs before it cooled too much. I realized I had an erection.

Maria unhooked her bra. "This is going to get soaked at this rate." Her breasts dwarfed Leah's. Together with her large upper arms, they gave an impression of power and grace in equal measure. With anyone else holding a pot of boiling water over me, I would have squirmed in fear.

The scalding water stopped dripping just as the warmth reached my shoulder blades. Maria put down the pot and picked up the cooler jockey. Then she started to pour the cool water onto me, dribbling it on my nipples. I jerked at the stabbing sensation. The icy streams ran down until they hit the warmth shrouding my back, then slowly dissipated against my sides. I ached from the intemperate zones Maria was creating on my body, and from awakening desire.

I growled and closed my eyes again, only to open them when freezing water hit my nose. Maria laughed. "We having fun yet? Tell me if I do anything you don't like." She picked up the crockpot and made steam rise right between my feet. My soles fizzed. Then the hot water stopped just as my balls were warming up again. I felt my frozen nipples being kissed by Maria. Her breath smelled like coffee. At that moment, it was the most luxurious smell in the world. Our mouths touched for a moment.

I still had an erection, but Maria hadn't acknowledged it. Until she picked up the blue bottle with one hand and the pot with the other. "They're light enough for me to do this now," she said, before tilting them both. Cold water hit the root of my prick and the crest of my scrotum, at the exact moment boiling water trickled between my legs, starting a fresh heat wave on my balls. I wriggled and let out a high groan. My cock softened, but not all the way. My brain couldn't process the warring pangs. "The contrast must be pretty intense," Maria said. "What does it feel like?"

"My cock and balls are in Alaska and Hawaii, respectively," I said through teeth. "They're talking on the phone, but there's a lot of interference."

"Let's see if we can improve the connection." Maria poured some of the cold water into the crockpot, then splashed the now-warm water on my cock. She brushed it gently with the loofah, and it cantilevered toward the sponge. The loofah ran over my cockhead and back down the side facing me. Then she splashed me again and my thirsty pelvis bucked against the flow.

"This isn't fair," I said. "You're doing all the work here. This bathtub's big enough for two."

"I thought you'd never ask." Maria had her birdie panties off in no time. Then she carefully put one foot on each of my shoulders before lowering her butt onto my thighs. "Now where did we put Mr. Loofah?" She fished between my legs, giving my balls a tweak before coming up with the tubular sponge. I took it from her and flicked it along the underside of her breasts and the top of her stomach. Maria made a cooing noise I'd never heard her make before. She tried to lean backwards but the faucets got in her way. So I helped her turn around and sat up so she could lean back against me. Cramped but comfortable enough. My cock nudged her as I ran the loofah up the back of her left arm, around the shaved armpit and back along the palm side until I carefully stroked each finger. I could just reach the crockpot without disturbing Maria, so I poured the warm water onto her breasts and stomach. I kept up the pouring motion while scrubbing her stomach with the loofah, until the pot was empty. Her stomach seemed as sensitive as her breasts, from the way she thrust it upwards. I leaned forward so my head was right on her neck, then sponged her thighs, stopping before I reached her vulva.

Maria wriggled her butt against me just as I was starting to get soft. I circled her snatch with the sponge, bringing it up to her chest and neck, then back down to her knees. I bit her ear experimentally, and it just made her wriggle harder. Our breathing deafened me in the echoing space. I started rubbing the sponge against her pubic bone, fibers against coarse hair. Worried the sponge might be too rough for direct contact, I slid my other hand directly onto her mound and stroked in a diminishing spiral. After a while, Maria turned again so she was facing me. She had a condom which I recognized from the stash under the sink. I took it and rolled it on quickly. Somehow she got her feet by my knees and her vulva directly over my cock, which she ground between her left thumb and two fingers for a moment until I got hard again. Her knees dug into my ribs, but I didn't care.

Then she lowered herself onto my cock. I exhaled slowly. Defenses I'd forgotten I'd put up fell away, floodwalls on bone-dry land. In their place, I felt a rawness from my throat down to my stomach. I saw Maria staring at my face. "Hey. How are you feeling?"

"OK. Relieved, I guess," I said. "I didn't realize how tense I'd been, keeping it together by sheer tightness. It's been kind of tough, watching my marriage fall apart." My eyes stung, and I realized I was actually crying.

"Do you want to talk about it?"

"I guess so. Wouldn't that be kind of a turn-off?"

"Not at all." Maria leaned forward and kissed me, so hard my tears wet her cheeks.

So I talked for a while about the hard stuff — abandonment, fear, future plans that had been swept away. It all poured out while Maria swayed on my dick and occasionally licked my cheekbones. Then she held me so tight I felt the forgotten loofah squeezed between us. I stopped talking and just cried quietly.

Then the tears ended, and I felt peaceful. Between the water below me and Maria on top of me, I felt submerged in warmth. I kissed Maria again, this time a slow caress. "It felt so good to talk," I said after a few moments. "Thank you."

"Any time."

We kept up the gentle pace for a bit, then Maria started to grind against me more, making waves. I sloshed water against her stomach and breasts with one hand and stroked what I could reach of her mound with the other. I felt so close to her at that moment, I would have given almost anything to make her feel good. We started a splash fight, me splashing her breasts and her splashing my ribs. I'm amazed there was any water left in the tub, so much had gone on the floor. We both started laughing, rubbing our bodies together in between splashing each other. I bit Maria's nose. She bit my chin. I shook my wet hair at her until her teeth let go. We giggled and thrashed. I remembered watching otters mate once at the aquarium, a slithery, rolling dance.

Just as my tongue entered Maria's mouth for the first time, our raindance paid off. I heard the pipes sing and water cascaded onto us. Strings hit me in the face and back from the showerhead above. Maria's feet had turned on the tap, I guess, and I found out much later a conscience-stricken Leah had paid the reconnection fees. At that moment, it seemed a miracle. The water froze us, but we kept fucking ever more joyously now that we were in a downpour. I had to blink away the water to look at Maria's shining face. Her mascara ran. She had her tongue out. "Yay!" She licked water off my face.

"It takes about two minutes for the water to get warm," I said. "Maybe more, since the heater's been idle a while."

"Who cares?" Maria gasped. "It's lovely!" We hugged each other for warmth as the shower pelted us.

By the time the water got warm, the walls and floor were soaked. I hardly cared that we hadn't closed the shower curtain, or that our frenzied otterfuck was deflecting water in all directions. I managed to dislodge the showerhead from its cheap holster by jerking on its metal-covered hose, then it fell and jerked in every direction until I grabbed it. Then I trained it on Maria's clit, which was under water by now. Her knees jabbed my ribs like spurs. With my other arm, I stroked the base of her spine, a down payment on her backrub. She ground into my pelvis, and I felt her muscles tighten around me. There wasn't enough lubrication to thrust any more, but I heard a noise from deep in her throat and she pressed harder against me. The overabundance of our joy seeped over the sides of the tub, we were no longer fucking but swimming against each other, and I held Maria so tight the showerhead was a second prick spurting endlessly between my pubic bone and hers.

OPTIONS
by Jacqueline Sinclaire

"Happy birthday to you…"

Her voice was low and sultry in my ear and I wondered when she would relieve me of this blindfold.

"Happy birthday to you!"

I felt her hand glide across my shoulders as she circled me, then her nails trailed up my neck and under my jaw before vanishing from my skin. I half wanted her to hurry up and finish the song while the other half wanted her to tease me until I died from anticipation.

"Happy birthday, dear Lynne…"

I was desperate to taste her, but I knew she was just beginning and my wait was far from over.

"Happy birthday… to… you."

This was my Caroline, my sweet, the love of my life, and she had been planning this for weeks, dropping little hints to drive me crazy. It was my 20th and she was determined to ring in this decade for me in a way I'd never forget. That was how I'd ended up in my current position, arms and legs tied to the chair; blindfold depriving me of my sight. I could still sense her though, and I knew she was aroused. I could smell her faintly. I knew her eyes were watching me, and I felt more exposed than I've ever been before, despite being fully clothed. She understood my body by now, knew the gentle slope of my petite breasts and the triangular patch of pubic hair I left above my snatch for ornamental reasons. She knew the easiest ways to make me come as well as how to hold me off until the last possible second.

There was a brief moment of silence once she finished the song, and I waited for something—*anything*—to happen. I thought I could feel her eyes burning holes through my clothes when I suddenly heard her footsteps leaving the room. The door closed slowly, and I sat there in amazement. *What was going on?*

"Caroline?" I called out. I was confused but also very wet from the possibilities.

"Patience, lover!" she called back, and my confusion dissolved into excitement. What in the world had this girl planned? Here I was, sitting blindly in the middle of her bedroom, still wearing my work clothes (black skirt, white blouse and no shoes) with my short red hair in wild disarrangement. My bare feet were getting cold on the hardwood floor, and I almost wished I could at least rub them together for warmth. Yet I was enjoying my bound, spread eagle position.

The door creaked slightly as it opened again and her footsteps sounded somewhat different. Louder and sharper. Was she wearing heels? I was shocked. Caroline is wild and naughty, but had never shown her attitude in her clothing. Sometimes she would wear these comfy knit shirts that shaped to her chest beautifully and revealed the shadow of an areola, but that was the extent of her experimentation with erotic outfits. She was a smart, comfortable dresser, steering clear of anything too extravagant. So the sudden realization that yes, she was wearing heels (stilettos by the sound of it!), topped with the question of "What else is she wearing?" made goose bumps appear all over my skin.

"I had to go get the rest of your gift," she explained as she reached me, her voice letting me know that she was standing a bit closer to me than I'd guessed.

I smiled in her direction... or, where I *thought* she was. She moved slightly and I realized I could feel her breath on my face.

"Now you have three options, followed by one mandatory choice. Being the good person that I am—" I didn't even have to see her smirk to know it was there— "You will experience all three of your options in the end, but you get to choose the order."

It took all of my will power not to move slightly and kiss her.

"You will only know your options as One, Two and Three. They are in no particular order, but are all equally exciting. You do, however, get to know what that last mandatory option is in advance." She moved in even closer and I could smell the soft scent of her skin. Her voice lowered to a whisper. "No matter what order you choose, you will definitely get fucked tonight."

With that said, she ran the tip of her tongue over my upper lip, pulling away before I could return the favor.

Three choices with one invariable result; I could not go wrong. "So what'll it be first?"

She was standing up again, waiting for my decision.

I licked my lips as I considered my options. They tasted like her.

"I suppose I'll go with number two first."

She chuckled softly.

"Good choice."

She stepped away from me, her heels click clacking across the floor. Again, that feeling of vulnerability washed over me, and I realized I didn't know I could feel this naked without actually being actually stripped bare. My loss of sight attributed to the sensation, as did my bound position, but I think a part of me *wanted* to feel so exposed. She had barely touched me, and I was already so turned on that I felt I could come at any moment.

I heard her rummaging with something on her… desk, yes that was in the direction she'd walked. There was silence, then the click-clack of her shoes as she made her way back to me.

For a second I thought my cell phone had gone off before I realized the buzzing was coming from whatever she had in her hands.

"As you've probably guessed, darling, behind door number two is a lovely new vibrator. Actually, a set of five."

Five? She got me five vibrators?

"Oh the wonders of Japanese technology" The buzzing sounded closer now. "They've invented these great finger attachments that will let me use my hands, with just a bit more of a punch than normal."

Her hand was so close to my neck that I could feel the air move slightly from the little mini vibes. She lowered the toy gently onto my skin for a split second just to give me an idea of the sensation.

"But to really experience this correctly, one must use them on bare skin." She told me this matter of factly while the hand without the vibrators slowly undid the buttons on my shirt. She left a few buttons at the bottom done up, moving quickly to expose only my breasts. I could feel my nipples pressing against the material of my black bra, hard and ready for her touch. Caroline tilted my head back and the blindfold moved slightly, but offered me no more of a view than before. Just the darkness, that hum and her touch.

The second time she touched me with the vibrators, I could feel the individual pulsations coming from each finger. She started at my neck, slowly moving down to my chest, sliding over the top of my left breast, circling around my still-covered nipple. The feel of the material of my bra coupled with the vibrations made my nipples ache with passion. She alternated breasts, still only touching very lightly. By the time she'd exposed my breasts from the cups with her other hand, I was panting from excitement.

"Well, it looks like *you're* having fun…"

I nodded my head before the vibrations reached my bare nipple. The shock threw my head back and made my hands grip the chair tightly. This was unlike anything I'd ever felt before, and I knew I was close to coming but I needed her hands elsewhere.

Without warning, she removed both her hands from me. I moaned; I was so close! My head hung limply on my chest and I desperately tried to at least press my thighs together for some sort of friction. No luck, my legs were tied firmly apart.

I heard her walk over to the desk again. On her way back, she spoke. My head wavered blindly in the direction of her voice.

"Time to choose again."

I choose to be put out of this torment, I thought, *to be in her arms and to make her want me as much as I wanted her right now*. But that wasn't an option yet.

"One."

My eyes were flooded with light as she finally removed the

blindfold. As I blinked rapidly, I realized that there wasn't much light in the room to begin with. She had lit a bunch of candles and… what was she wearing?

My beautiful Caroline, most comfortable in khakis, was dressed in a black skintight PVC mini dress, thigh-high fishnet stockings, towering stilettos, and black latex gloves that went past her elbows. Her blonde curls were loose and wild. She must have just put the gloves on because I would have noticed them against my skin. Her green eyes glittered mischievously as she waited for me to take in her total transformation. The dress flattered her ample breasts and juicy ass, cutting off midthigh before showing any cheek, though with a little movement it would probably reveal a lot more.

She turned and walked over to the stereo. I watched, mesmerized. Every step was a redefinition of the sexiest thing I'd ever seen. She reached out with that shiny, gloved hand to press the "play" button. A soft song came on, low and sultry, and I faintly recognized the melody. It was some band from Montreal.

Walking back towards me, she gave me a wink and spoke. "Option number one is a striptease."

She closed her eyes for a second before beginning. Her body moved slowly, languidly, and just as I'd fantasized, the dress crept up as she danced. She came right up to me, her hands gliding across her chest, down her hips and then back up to her inner thighs. I got a quick glimpse of bright red panties and moaned at the mere sight of them. I was beyond aroused and yet I knew I still had one more door to open, one more choice to make.

She repeated these motions, in varying order, before her hands finally moved to the zipper at the top of the dress and pulled it down inch by inch by inch, so her bare chest was viewable to me. I could tell this was as much a turn on for her as it was for me. Her eyes were closed and her body moved slowly and sensuously. She was the most amazing creature I'd ever seen.

Straddling me on the chair, she ground herself into me. Her skirt had already ridden up past her ass, and the motion of her body pulled mine up to expose my well-soaked panties. She smelled delectable, and I leaned forward to kiss her. But she pulled away and while still gyrating on me, leant back until her head almost touched the ground behind her. Her body formed a perfect arch and her breasts slid past the material of her dress. Her nipples hardened as the cool air touched them, and I longed to envelop them in my mouth.

She sat up swiftly and lifted her weight off me as she stood. After undoing the rest of her zipper and letting the dress fall to the floor, my beautiful Caroline was exposed at last. Her skin was golden brown, like a pot of honey and just as sweet. With curves from Victorian times, my large-bosomed beauty gracefully twirled and dipped for me. Slipping behind me swiftly, her hands snaked around my waist, then down my thighs, to my knees, then back up again. The feel of the latex gloves against my skin was exquisite, as was the contrast between my pale thighs and their inky blackness. As she stroked my skin she whispered to me, "Looks like we've just got number three to do now."

I nodded, hoping it involved the release of this ache between my thighs.

She moved in front of me again and we both surveyed each other. She was still wearing those darling red panties, the stockings, shoes and gloves. I knew I looked a mess, skirt hitched up almost to my waist, blouse half open and my breasts pushed out above my bra. By the look in her eyes I knew she had me just the way she wanted me.

Wandering over to her desk yet again, she returned with something new in her hands. A beautiful blue dildo.

"This…" she waved it a bit "is not for you. Yet." Her smile was pure sex and wickedness. "This is for me, and for you to watch."

She backed towards the bed, then sat down and began to caress her breasts, stomach, and thighs. Finally, she slid her free hand down her panties. As she touched herself, I honestly believed I would tear the chair to bits before the night was over. My hands only clenched the armrest tighter as she kept going. I watched, transfixed, as she removed her hand from her panties just long enough to take them off. Then she lay back on the bed, completely exposing herself to me. Her beautiful shaved pussy was on display for my viewing pleasure.

I knew how to make her come but I had never really watched her do it herself. She didn't even bother to take off the gloves, and I wondered what they felt like on her skin, on her wet pussy lips.

She brought the dildo close to her pussy, then she spread her lips and played the blue dildo over her slit. She slipped just a bit in, then pulled it out and rubbed the tip all over her clit. I could see how wet she was getting and this only made me wetter too. She pushed the dildo all the way in with one quick thrust, and her moan was the most glorious music I'd ever heard. I ground my pussy into the chair, looking for any kind of friction at all.

She thrust the dildo into herself hard and fast while playing with her clit. I knew she was getting close, her pussy was tightening and her breathing grew heavier and heavier.

"Lynne?" Her voice trembled when she called out my name. "I wish this was you..."

I groaned from her words and watched as she finally let go. Her cries were loud and delirious, her hips raised off the bed. I could almost feel her pussy contracting, could almost taste the juices flowing from her.

I waited for her to regain her senses as patiently as I could, considering the condition I was in. Slowly, ever so slowly, she sat up a bit and pulled the dildo out, her hands still trembling a bit from the staggering orgasm.

It was only because of the surprised look she gave me that I realized I was whimpering from my need. "Caroline, I want to come."

Grinding my hips futilely against my seat just wasn't going to work. She moved quickly over to me, starting to take off the gloves.

"No!" I was almost frantic. "Leave them on."

She smiled as she knelt before me and started to undo the knots. Her lips finally found my own and she tasted like wine and candy and fruits I couldn't name. Her hands worked quickly and in a matter of seconds she had untied me.

She didn't pull away from my mouth as she slowly raised me out of the chair and onto the bed. My limbs slowly stretched out and relaxed, happy to be free from that chair. The relief was short lived, as my lust became even stronger than before. I began to move my hand down to finish myself off but she stopped me, the feel of the glove against my skin completely new. She put my hands at my sides and then worked at removing the rest of my clothing until I was finally as naked as I'd felt the whole time.

Once again, she trailed her fingers over my skin, this time clad in smooth latex. She caressed my body and built up my passion again to its boiling point. By the time she'd reached my clit, just a few quick rubs sent me over the edge. I came, screaming her name in one of the best orgasms of my life.

As I lay there, slowly coming down to earth, I reached over and took hold of the hand she'd used on herself. I slowly licked every drop of her off the slick material, enjoying her flavor immensely.

Realizing I hadn't opened my eyes, I did so and found her staring at me adoringly. Uh oh. She wasn't done with me yet. She still had something up her sleeves, or latex gloves, as it were.

Caroline moved her hand back between my thighs and slipped a single finger inside me. There was than enough natural lube to work with so another finger went in easily enough. She pulled out very slowly before thrusting back in fast and hard. Just how I liked it. With every thrust, she pressed against my g-spot and her thumb brushed my clit roughly. With that combination, I wasn't able to hold out for long.

She muffled my cries with her mouth as I came the second time, my hips bucking wildly. She didn't even let me recover. Her hand kept the pace and I had my third orgasm not even a minute later, collapsing, completely exhausted from the whole experience.

She took off the gloves, then her heels before lying down beside me and covering us with the duvet. I was still lightheaded from it all.

I looked into her grass green eyes, completely in love and in lust with this woman. She just smiled and asked, "Well, how was that for a birthday present?"

I laughed and pulled her body closer to mine.

"I think that was a birthday to remember."

PURE SIN
by Sheri Gilmore

"Harder. Harder!"

Muscles burned. Teeth ground tight.

"Put your ass into it, Georgie."

George Chen's gaze narrowed on the plump blonde, and a trickle of sweat slid down his forehead. He lunged forward, pounding deeper.

"That's it. That's it!" Her eyes closed while short fingernails dug into his forearm.

A smile touched the corner of his mouth.

"Yes, yes, yes!"

George focused. A lock of hair escaped the tight queue at the nape of his neck. Mixed with the sweat on his skin, it clung to his face.

The blonde's fingers relaxed. "Perrrfect, darling."

The satisfaction in her voice slowed his questing fingers until he let them slide and stroke through the sticky sweetness before him.

"Stop." She pushed at his hand. "Stop. That's too much!"

George rolled his eyes to the ceiling, then back to the woman. He leaned close.

"Dixie, you drive a man crazy."

She smiled and patted his arm. "That's why your brother married me."

My God. Tess Mikel watched the man's arm muscles work, his powerful hands kneading the dough back and forth. She was close to an orgasm, sitting on the edge of her stool, thigh and abdominal muscles clenched. Her body throbbed, but she continued to watch the couple's reflection in the shop window. The crotch of her panties grew moist, listening to the girl's seductive words.

Tess closed her eyes as she imagined the feel of those hands on her skin. Tiny puffs of air escaped her lips. She forced her body to relax. The man was pure sin.

She drank her coffee, alone, in the little bakery, watching him as she had every workday for the past month. Monday through Friday. And every day, like today, he'd made her body hot, aching with a desire none of her past boyfriends had ever evoked. He was her secret fantasy.

Her eyes traveled over his reflection. Her skin tingled at the sight. Long, black hair caught in a ponytail along a muscle-corded neck, one stray strand clinging to his skin. She wanted to nip the black silkiness with her teeth.

Tess squirmed on her seat, crossing her legs to ease the familiar ache. Dregs from her paper coffee cup sloshed to the table. Her hands shook with the desire to rip the tank top from his body and sink her teeth into his toned muscles.

He stacked some doughnut boxes under the counter, his back to her.

What an amazing ass. She glanced around the shop, frightened the other customers could hear her thoughts. Tess bit her lip. He'd never know she was in love with him. She couldn't sleep with dreams of him. Her concentration at work was nil.

The paper cup crushed beneath her fingers. She looked away from the object of her desire. She was pitiful, lusting after the doughnut boy.

She peeked at her watch, her pulse racing. If she didn't get moving she was going to be late. With one last furtive glance at the window, her head shook in denial. *Boy?* The reflection mirrored six-feet-four inches of muscled steel.

Unwillingly, her gaze traced the green-and-red dragon tattoo circling one bicep. She swallowed. He was all man. *Dark.* She crushed her napkin, her heart accelerating. *Dangerous.*

Dixie tapped George with the toe of her shoe. "Attack at three o'clock."

Behind the counter, George stilled. Then, stacking the last of the doughnut boxes on the shelf, he rose, the hair on the back of his neck tingled. Great, this was all he needed.

"Hi, George."

He turned to a high-pitched feminine voice and gave his best business smile.

"Hey, how are you?" He tried to remember the buxom redhead's name, a woman who he'd screwed a few months before, but couldn't.

"What can I get you today?"

The woman leaned barely-concealed breasts across the counter, letting George have free view of her cleavage.

His mouth filled with saliva. With an effort, he lifted his gaze to the woman's face.

"Well, since you asked. You can *dough* me right," she said, quoting the bakery's catchy title, 'Dough Me Right Doughnuts.' Her smile was wide and inviting. She giggled with a shimmy of her shoulders. Boobs jiggled in the tight-knit shirt.

Damn. George's gaze stared straight ahead. He'd promised his brother, owner of the shop, he was finished fraternizing with female customers. It was just—he looked down and almost groaned at the sight of the perky breasts begging him—so hard.

From the corner of his eye he caught a movement. If he turned his head just an inch, he'd see the one woman he'd never spoken to. Tall and willowy, she wasn't his usual type, but he'd been watching her for the last month. Wanting her.

She stood, wadding her paper cup and napkin before placing them into the waste can. Her every movement drew his attention. Graceful. Flowing. Like a ballet dancer.

His cock hardened. He'd always had a secret fantasy for ballet dancers.

"Excuse me."

George swung his gaze away from his ballerina to "the exotic dancer." His imagination's contrast between the two women made him grin.

"Yeah?" He cleared his throat. "What can I get you?"

"Ohhh. Never mind." The redhead turned from watching his slender ballerina slip through the door. She glared at him and stomped off.

George shrugged and let his gaze track the more tantalizing woman like a wolf. His eyes narrowed at the way the material of her long skirt clung to shapely legs.

His mouth dry, he leaned his elbows on the counter. The bell above the door jingled and his fantasy woman disappeared until next week. She didn't show on the weekends, only during the week on her way to work.

Images of long legs wrapped tight around his waist and back skirted the edges of his mind. He could almost feel his cock driving deeper into her body. Sweat broke across his brow. That sweet, little ass. He groaned.

"Fat chance, buddy," said Dixie. She threw him a wet rag. "She's out of your league."

"Thanks a lot, Dix." He grabbed the towel, moving to the end the counter closest to the table where she'd sat. He wiped the counter, the frustration of the last month building in his gut. Ballerinas wouldn't look twice at guys like him.

His glance fell on the set of keys tucked under her chair. He grinned. Or, would they?

Tess inhaled cold New York City air. She crossed the street to catch the subway to work, glancing left and right for traffic. Forget him. Forget him. The words were her daily mantra. People getting on the train jostled her from every angle, but she didn't notice.

It was useless to waste her energy on a man who obviously preferred the more earthy types of women like the one she'd seen blatantly flirting with him. Women with large breasts and skin-tight clothing. Maybe she could—

No way. Tess grabbed a leather handle above her head. Even if she got enough nerve to approach him, she wouldn't ever wear such provocative clothing. Her conservative cohorts at the bank would have heart failure. Not to mention her uptight family.

She glanced down at her clothes. A white, silk blouse tucked neatly into a loose blue skirt. She shrugged and lifted her head in self-defense.

Her clothes were... stylish. She glanced down again. Comfortable.

Her heart sank. Boring.

Her hand touched her hair. Her face. She flinched inwardly. She pictured long, dull-brown hair swept into a chignon and a face without makeup, except a swift pass of a mascara wand. These were boring, too. Tess pursed her lips and glanced out the window. She wished she could come out of her shell. Her head bowed with naughty thoughts of her fantasy man.

"Excuse me, but I think this belongs to you," said a deep, masculine voice.

Tess turned towards the voice. Her heart stopped. It was him.

The surprise she felt melted into confusion as she registered the object he held towards her. Her key ring. "I must have left them," she said. *Great deduction, Tess.*

"Thank you." She released the train's handgrip and reached for the keys, embarrassment preventing her from looking directly into his face.

Her fingers closed over the cool metal ring at the same moment the train lurched. Thrown forward into a solid wall of heat, her breath caught.

Strong arms wrapped around her body as the scent of clean, male sweat and baked bread engulfed her senses. She closed her eyes and breathed deeply.

When she opened her eyes, the heat of his gaze pierced her. Tiny arrows of desire spread across her abdomen until they settled in the nerve endings of her clit. Moisture and heat pooled. She moved her hips to ease the pressure, rubbing against the front of his jeans by accident. She thought she heard him groan.

His head lowered, as if in slow motion. His mouth covered hers with lips like molten lava, scorching her to her soul. Tess gasped and he took advantage, his tongue circling hers. He tasted like coffee, rich and dark. With a moan, Tess let her hands snake around his neck to draw him closer. The sensation of drowning spread. Nothing mattered except the feel of his mouth on hers.

Somewhere in the distance Tess heard a cough. She frowned. The sound was aggravating in her world of hot flames, licking and caressing. Stroking—

"Ahem." The cough was louder and closer to her ear.

"Would you two take that somewhere else so we less fortunate creatures can get off the train and go to our humdrum jobs?"

Tess stiffened. She pulled her lips away from the brief heaven she'd known. Head bowed, she opened her eyes, reluctantly, hoping to keep reality's vengeance at bay.

Fat chance.

A bald guy, eating a bagel, winked at her from her left, eyebrows twitching up and down.

Tess turned quickly to her right. An older woman with a brown, grocery sack, glared at her. The woman clutched the sack to her chest and pushed around them. When she reached the other side, she swung the purse she also held, connecting with her fantasy man's arm.

He grunted at the impact.

"Yeah, buddy, get a room," echoed around them.

Tess stared at the floor. Heat scorched her neck and cheeks. She couldn't move. Good girls didn't act this way. *She* didn't act this way.

The arms around her tightened, but she refused to look up. Warm breath tickled her ear, causing tiny shivers of desire to travel down her neck.

"What's wrong, princess? Don't you like a little exhibitionism?" His voice was liquid heat.

She closed her eyes and melted into the sound. "Yes," she said before she could help herself. With a start she looked up. He wasn't supposed to know her fantasies. What was he doing to her?

Tess pulled out of his arms and followed the throng of people, making their way from the subway into the bright sunshine of the bustling street. She looked around, blinking at the sudden glare, trying to get a point of reference. Tall buildings. Traffic. The gates to Liberty Park.

A wave of relief washed over her. She wasn't insane. The ride on the subway had thrown her into the "Twilight Zone" for a short period.

"Hey!" She raised her arm to signal one of the cabbies hovering nearby. She glanced at her watch. She was really late for work. "Hey!"

"Spend the day with me."

Tess twisted her body towards the deep voice behind her, pain shooting into her ankle. "Ouch!" She stumbled and grabbed her ankle.

Immediately, he was beside her. Warm, tan fingers ran the length of her lower leg, pushing her hands away from her ankle. "Let me help you."

"No, no, that's okay," she said. The tingling sensation his touch generated made her clench her teeth so tight her jaw hurt. His contact was harder to bear than that of her injury.

Their hands bumped and entwined as each fought for the right to rub her leg until Tess caught his hands.

"Please stop," she said.

Dark eyes glittered. Desire held her motionless. They stared at each other for what seemed an eternity. A slow, sexy grin spread across the stranger's face. He looked like a bad, little boy.

Tess blinked in surprise at the transformation. Except—she grinned back—he wasn't a stranger. He was the gorgeous man she had wanted for a month. Still wanted. Fingers trembled as she gingerly stood and held out her hand. "Hi."

One black eyebrow arched before he took her hand in his. "Hi, yourself."

Her fingers squeezed his. Their hands dropped between their bodies, swinging back and forth like two kids holding hands on a field trip.

"I'm Tess. Tess Mikel."

"Tess?" He exerted pressure against her hand, pulling her closer.

She nodded. "Short for Teresa, but everyone calls me…" She let the words fade. Her breath caught deep in her lungs.

He pulled her closer still. With his free hand, he skimmed

fingertips over her face and hair, while his eyes devoured her. "I like the name Teresa."

A hand tunneled under her hair, spilling pins over the concrete. When his face blotted out the sunshine, Tess knew he was going to kiss her again. She closed her eyes. Butterflies danced in her belly. His lips were light, not the mind-blowing encounter of earlier, but just as effective at confusing her. He leaned his forehead against hers.

"I'm George." He kissed her nose. "And I'm going to make love to you."

Tess wasn't sure she'd heard him correctly, except the heat in his gaze told her otherwise.

"Now," he said.

Her knees trembled so badly, if he hadn't been holding her, she would have fallen. The tattoo of her heart pounded so hard against her chest she thought everyone in New York City could hear it.

George kept one hand on Tess and raised the other to hail a taxi. Careful of her ankle, he assisted her into the cab. When she was settled in the back seat, he studied her—eyes slightly glazed with passion. Breathing rapid. Long hair wild around her shoulders.

He pulled her close, a smile tugging at his mouth. She was far from being a prim and proper ballerina at the moment. He intended keeping her dazed for a while longer.

"George?"

"Don't talk, just feel." His fingers stroked her arm through the silk blouse. The soft, smooth sensation against the callused nerve endings of his fingers vibrated through his arm and body into his cock. He moved his hand to the front of her blouse, letting his fingertips feather across her breast. Her body stiffened.

"Shh, baby. Relax," he said against her hair before his tongue wove a trail from her temple to her ear. He flicked his tongue inside, prepared when her body jumped at the contact. He tightened his palm over her breast. She whimpered. The sound of her helpless reaction sent shivers down his spine. His right hand traveled over her delicate ankle, inching upwards. With deft fingers, he waded through the layers of her skirt until he reached her thigh. His hand faltered.

He turned her face to his and let his tongue trace her lips. "Good, girls don't wear thigh highs, Tess." He snapped the elastic against her skin, liking the sharp 'pop' it made. "Will you be bad for me?"

Her eyes widened. A deep moan escaped her parted lips at the same time she parted her legs to give him easier access to the heat his fingers searched for.

George traced the edge of her panties, all the time watching her face. "I'm going to make you come here in this cab." He pushed the material aside enough to tease her pussy, barely dipping in and out of her moist folds. Her musky scent rose to tease his nostrils.

The muscles of her thighs tightened around his hand. She hesitated. Her eyes searched his before glancing towards their driver. A dusky shade of pink tinged her cheeks, but she buried her head against his shoulder and nodded her assent.
George's cock tightened. He pulled her head up into a deep kiss and plunged two fingers inside her. His thumb worked her clit. Stroking. Pressing.

Fingernails stabbed his shoulders. Within seconds, her body arched against his and he swallowed her cry of release with his mouth. Damp hair wrapped around her face from exertion. George pulled the strands away with his free hand. He kissed her nose and forehead, making shushing sounds to calm her. George felt the driver's stare, but he continued to play in the moist heat of her cunt. Tess' eyes were bright with excitement. She knew they were being observed. He grew harder.

"You're a bad girl, Tess. I'm going to have to punish you."

Tess heard herself moan, but couldn't stop the sound. George moved his fingers inside her. Pressure built to the point of pain, but its fruition was something she wouldn't deny herself. She needed this. She flung her head back.

"Yes, yessss." Screams of her second orgasm echoed through the cab.

She felt George's cock lengthen against her thigh. Tess glanced into the mirror and met his smug gaze, then, her eyes clashed with the cabby's. His eyes were wide and full of desire. A flood of moisture eased between her legs.

George's fingers moved deeper inside her body. "That's right, baby, come for us one more time," he said. "We've only got eyes for you, Tess."

By the time they reached his curb, she was screaming his name, pumping her hips against his hand for a third climax. "Geooorge!"

He wrapped his arms around her and held her trembling body to him, his breathing hard and fast. Tess heard him give a shaky laugh. He kissed her and turned her face towards the cabby, who watched her with sated eyes.

"I think you made him come. You like that?" he asked, his fingers stroking her cheek.

She experienced a moment of shyness, but she didn't pull away. Instead, she buried her face against George's body, which was damp from the heat of his own excitement, and nodded. A wave of exhaustion hit her.

"How much do I owe you?" George's voice sounded far away.

"Nothin'. The 'ride's' on me," said the cabby.

George grinned, acknowledging the other man's pleasure. He lifted Tess in his arms, helping her to his apartment. Between a twisted ankle and three orgasms, she must be wiped out.

He unlocked the door and stepped over the threshold like a groom carrying his bride. He frowned at the analogy and slammed the door with one foot.

Her breathing was deep and her face was relaxed. He took her to his bed and laid her down. The comforter rustled under her slender body.

His ballerina. Tenderness and possessiveness washed over him as he watched her. Powerful emotions. He was in love with a fantasy. One who appeared to be fast asleep.

George stepped away from the bed. The need to run was overwhelming. It wasn't love. *Was* it? He watched the outline of her breasts as she breathed, then, turned away and shook his head. *Just because we had kinky sex doesn't mean it wasn't love—*

"Who are you talking to?"

He hadn't realized he'd spoken out loud. He looked at her

quickly, and she smiled, watching him with drowsy eyes. Her body stretched like a lazy cat. "Come to bed, then, and let's do some more kinky stuff."

His heart skipped a beat. "You enjoyed what we did in the cab?"

Her cheeks grew pink, her smile wavered, but she held his gaze. She swallowed hard. "I—That's always been kind of a fantasy of mine."

He couldn't believe his luck. He'd found the woman of his dreams. "Any more fantasies I can help you with?"

She cocked her head and grinned. "I guess that I'd like you to 'dough me right'."

He arched his eyebrow. "You, imp." He grabbed her and tickled her ribs. "I've already 'doughed' you." His body captured hers and he kissed her hard before easing into a playful nip.

"But, I'll be glad to *do* you again. Anyway you want."

QUICK FIX
by Heather Peltier

I don't know why; sometimes it just happens. Some fluctuation of my hormones or something that makes me think about you all morning. I'm squirming in my desk, feeling that tingling all over my body that tells me if I don't satisfy the need building inside me, I'm going to go absolutely crazy.

Normally, I hold it. I mean, I just put it out of my mind, bringing it back out between meetings, when I'm sitting at my desk answering voice mail messages. I sit there and think about you while some lower-level manager is telling me her problems, blathering on about one thing or another. I sit there and get wet thinking about you, but I don't do anything about it. I don't rush home and fuck you, no matter how badly I want to.

This time, though, I can't sit still. I can't handle it. Sitting in meetings, all I can think about is you: your lips, pressed against mine; your tongue, pressing urgently into my mouth; your chest, thrusting hard against me, teasing my nipples with your soft hair; and, most importantly, your glorious cock, sliding between my lips while I kneel in front of you, or sinking deep into me as you enter me.

I call you on your cell phone. I know you'll answer, because you're on a job, in the middle of construction on a half-million dollar home up in the hills.

"Are you free for lunch?" I ask you breathlessly.

"Sure," you say. "Everyone else is going down to the deli, but I can meet you someplace."

Our home is more than 20 minutes away, but the construction site is only 10. "No," I tell you. "Stay right where you are. Give me the address."

"I'm a little tight on time," you say. "We'll have to go somewhere close."

"I'll bring something to eat," I tell you.

"Oh, a picnic," you say.

"You could say that."

I call my client's cell phone and cancel our lunch meeting.

Hit with pangs of guilt, I grab an apple off my desk and stuff it into the pocket of my business suit. I make a quick stop in the restroom, race out the door of my office and hop into my car.

Seven minutes later, I find you sitting on the unfinished wooden steps of the house, reading a paperback.

"Hi," you smile. "Did you bring food?"

"I brought something to eat," I tell you, taking your hand. "Is anyone else here?"

"Everyone else is down at the deli," you say, looking at me suspiciously. "What are you up to?"

I walk into the construction site, seeing you start to say something. You've said it before: I'm not on your payroll, so you're risking serious insurance consequences if you let me on your site. But this time, I'm not taking no for an answer.

"Nice place you've got here," I say, walking through what I suppose will be the entryway. Most of the walls are nothing more than two-by-fours, unfinished plywood nail-gunned up to keep the vagrants out. I walk deeper into the house-inprogress and find the kitchen.

You're tagging along behind me. I shrug off my blazer and toss it on a sawdust-covered belt sander. I reach up and unclip my hair, letting it fall in a dark curtain all around my shoulders and face as I run my fingers through it.

"Hey," you say. "You really shouldn't be hanging out in here..."

I turn around and face you, smiling.

"I don't intend to hang out anywhere," I say, and slowly unzip my conservative navy-blue skirt.

It falls in a pool around my feet, and I step out of it.

On my top half, I'm now wearing only my skintight pale yellow camisole, no bra underneath. I'm small enough that I don't need to wear one — as long as I don't take off my blazer. Now that it's off, I can feel the cool air of the dark construction site brushing my nipples, which are standing out, peaked and firm, aching. On my bottom half, I'm wearing only a pair of lace-top white stockings, hitched to my garter belt with thin white garters and businesslike navy pumps with three-inch heels. My pussy, feeling slick and messy with the juice of wanting you, is bare. My panties are tucked in the top drawer of my desk. I removed them before coming over.

"I need a quick fix," I tell you, reaching between my legs and gently teasing my pussy. "Very quick."

Glancing around, you see that we're close to several open areas that passersby might be able to see through. You look from me to the street, then to me again.

I lift my hand to my face, slipping my finger into my mouth. I've been playing with my pussy and it tastes like me. And you know it. I lick my finger sensuously, and that's all it takes. You come for me.

I'm down on my knees before you reach me. I've got your filthy, paint-stained work pants open in a split second, and I reach in to pull out your cock. When I take it into my mouth, it's only half-hard. By the time it reaches the back of my throat, it's hard all the way.

I feel a quiver go through you as I swallow your cock. You moan softly as I pump it into me, feeling the sawdust and fragments of plasterboard abrading my knees, tearing my stockings. The roughness of the environment turns me on even more, as does the smell of fresh sawdust and the street noise so close to us, making me feel exposed and vulnerable as I suck you. Vulnerable to humiliation, because I know if you get caught you'll be in big, big trouble. Supervisor or not, you're not supposed to be doing that. That knowledge sends a surge of excitement through me as your hips began to rock back and forth, pushing your cock deeper into my mouth, deeper into my throat. I caress your balls with my fingers, coaxing you into greater thrusts, fucking me as I kneel in front of you.

You grasp my hair and pull me back gently; my mouth keeps working, inches from your glistening cockhead, my tongue aching to touch you more, my throat open and hungry for your shaft. I look up at you, at your beautiful dark eyes.

"I'm going to come if you don't stop," you tell me. "I want you on the counter."

You gesture toward the skeletal beginnings of a built-in kitchen island. Obediently, I stand up and bend over it, leaning fully on it so my legs leave the ground and my ass hovers in the air, my legs dangling helplessly and my pussy exposed. Now that I'm higher, off the ground, I'm acutely aware of the unfinished windows, bare emptiness facing what will be the back yard, what will be the side. The street noise excites me; almost anyone could look in, if they just walked on to the unprotected site.

"Close your eyes," you tell me, and I do.

I'm full of surprises; I guess you know that. But I don't think I gave you enough credit for being the same, because what I feel next sends a shiver through my body.

You've grabbed some rope. You wrap it around my wrist and start to tie me to the island.

I hear myself gasping; I feel my whole body tensing as I realize that you've pushed this so much further than I intended to go. I feel the sharp pang of fear deep in my body giving rise to a slow pulse of desire as I feel you quickly, expertly knotting the ropes around my wrists, tying me to the skeletal frame of the unfinished kitchen island. I don't struggle at first; I feel safe with you. Then, when I test the bonds and feel how tight you've tied them, I feel a rush of excitement and fear mingling deep in my pussy. It floods wet and I can practically feel it dripping down my inner thighs. When I pull against the bonds, squirming and struggling, you grab firm hold of my leg and that excites me more. Forcing my legs apart, you quickly tie first one ankle, then the other, to the framework of the island.

When I test the bonds, I find myself immobile. I'm helpless, bent over, ass in the air, spread, vulnerable. Anyone could walk in here and have me. And you know it.

As I squirm, I feel my hard nipples rubbing against the rough plywood under me. They hurt a little from the roughness, but strangely I don't mind it. I want it more. The more I squirm, the more my nipples ache and tingle. Meanwhile, I feel your hand on my ass — and it's not empty. You're holding a sander.

You barely press at all as you draw the sandpaper slowly down the backs of my thighs, then over my smooth, slim ass. I catch my breath, overwhelmed with sensation: With the dusty smell of the ropes, the sharp tang of sawdust and plywood, the scent of your sweat-soaked, unwashed body, the sound of the street so close by, the cool breeze through the open framework of the house. The heat of my pussy as you bend close to me and put your mouth against the back of my neck.

"I've been wondering how to reward my men for working so hard," you growl into my hear, and my back stiffens, my pussy flooding with heat as you torment me. I feel one hand grinding the sandpaper very lightly against my ass and thighs, the other hand pressing against my pussy and clit. Two fingers enter me, and I gasp. "A monetary bonus just didn't seem like it would satisfy them. How kind of you to provide the perfect reward for a hard day's work."

The heat rises in my pussy as I push back onto you, your fingers pumping me as your growl intensifies, your breath hot and the smell of your sweat close in my nostrils.

"How about if I just leave you here and let them use you for as long as they like? We wouldn't get much work done this afternoon, but I'm sure they'd work twice as hard tomorrow."

I moan softly, writhing in the bonds, pushing back onto you as hard as I can as you fingerfuck me. Your cock still hangs out of your open pants, still moist with my spittle, still hard. When you ease your fingers out of my pussy and toss the sandpaper away, I know what's coming.

"Think you could handle that?" you ask me. "There are 15 of them."

That sends a shiver through me as you position yourself behind me, your cock finding the slick furrow between my pussy lips without delay. You enter me in one hard thrust, and I'm so open I take you all, gasping as your cock hits my G-spot. I squirm and try to press back onto you, but your weight bears me down, and the bonds keep me firmly in place. As you start to pound me, my nipples rub raw against the plywood, through the thin silk of my camisole. My hips press into the edge of the wood; I can feel my flesh scraping, but I'm not worrying about splinters. I'm imagining all your workmen fucking me, even as your cock begins to plumb my depths faster and faster with each thrust.

"Come on," you sigh. "You don't mind contributing a little extra to the family business, do you, honey?"

Your cock is hitting exactly the right spot; it always does when you fuck me in this position. From behind, I mean — you've never fucked me in a construction site while I'm bent over a half-done counter. But you know what angle is the perfect one to shove your cock into me, and your cockhead is rubbing me in just the right place to make me...

Come.

But I don't, yet, not quite; you seem to sense I'm closing in on it and slow down just enough to keep me hovering on the edge.

"Say you'll do it, honey," you say, tormenting me with the slowness of your thrusts. "Say you'll let my men use you."

I want to come so bad I would say anything to make you fuck me harder. "Oh God," I gasp. "Of course I will. Of course I will. Anything you want."

"All of them?"

"All of them," I whimper, straining against the bonds and trying to force myself back onto your cock, harder. "Every last one. I'll fuck them all... oh God —"

You start pounding into me again, the head of your cock striking my G-spot in exactly the way it takes to send me over the edge. You grip my slender thighs and hold me down as you ravage me, your cock pumping deep into my cunt and wrenching my orgasm from me.

"Oh God," I moan. "I'm going to —"

Then I do, uncontrollably, your cock savaging me with every

thrust, invading me, possessing me. I come so hard my eyes go dim, my whole body goes numb except my exploding clit, my pulsing pussy. I moan, helpless, not even caring who on the street can hear me, bound and naked, getting fucked in a kitchen where rich people will make their California Cuisine. Toward the end I hear myself screaming, as the intensity of my orgasm gets to be more than I can handle. And still you pound me, forcing me to handle it, forcing me to take it, forcing me to experience the most intense orgasm of my life. An orgasm so intense I'm afraid, for a moment, I'm going to pass out.

Then I hear you moaning, feel your cock clenching, feel the thick flood of semen that spells your release. I moan softly, savoring the feel of wetness that comes when you fill me. I lay there, immobile, bent over, exposed, bound — your slave. A bonus for your men, or whoever else you want to possess me.

You slip out of my pussy, your cock softening in its post-coital satisfaction. A thin stream of your come starts to leak down my thigh; it makes me shiver to feel it.

You make short work of the knots on my wrists and ankles. You help me down off the counter and hand me my skirt. My arms go around you and you hug me close, kissing the top of my head.

"What," I say. "No bonus for your men?"

"Nope," you tell me. "I'm keeping this one all to myself."

ROSE'S VIBRATOR
by M. Christian

Currently located in the drawer in Rose—short for Roseanna—and Patrick's—not really short for anything—bedside table, I am a Rabbit Pearl vibrator, a tubular pink plastic device 5 inches long, 1-1/2 inches wide, used for the enhancement of sexual pleasure. Manufactured in Japan out of durable vinyl, I was purchased for approximately $90 from Good Vibrations while the couple vacationed in San Francisco. It was my first impression that I was selected from among other similar devices for my "playful"—according to Rose—and nonthreatening—unspoken but clear from Patrick—appearance.

Indicative of my design and construction in Japan, which customarily does not create dildos that actually look like penises, I resemble less a realistic depiction of a phallus than I do a harmless toy. About halfway down my main shaft, for example, is a ring of several dozen plastic pearls, which energetically vibrate when I am activated. Continuing my "playful" design scheme, anchored below this band, is what appears to be a comic representation of a rabbit, with fluttering ears to stimulate the clitoris—thus the English interpretation of my Japanese name.

In addition to the rabbit component's buzzing ears, I also vibrate and oscillate, thanks to a special mechanical arrangement in my shaft that gently corkscrews. All of this—the buzzing bunny ears, the vibrating shaft, the ring of beads—is controlled by a simple mechanism at the end of a thin power cord.

For a few days after my sale to Rose and Patrick, I felt that my purpose was going to go unappreciated, as—still wrapped in brown paper—I was exiled to the bottom of an overstuffed suitcase. This puzzled me because while I noted a certain discomfort from Patrick as he lifted me off a shelf and laughed at my bunny and beads, I also noticed a special twinkle in Rose's very curious eyes.

A day or so and several hundred miles later, I was pleasantly surprised when the darkness around me disappeared, and I saw those same sparkling green eyes again. "Come on, let's try it," Rose said.

Batteries were inserted into my control box and, with a slide of one of my switches, I was turned on. Rose giggled, nearly hysterically. Patrick, though, was obviously less enamored of me than his girlfriend. It was at that moment, she laughing, he smiling but tense, that I decided I would be Rose's vibrator.

"Here," she said, as she slipped off her t-shirt. "Touch me with it." Reaching down, she cupped a small but beautifully perky breast, pointing a dark, rosy nipple out at him.

Cautiously, he reached out with me, grazing the hardened knot with my gently buzzing head. At the contact, she squealed delightfully and jumped back a bit, palm sliding between my plastic and her breast.

"Oh—I'm sorry," he said, turning me off.

"No, no—just a bit of a shock, that's all. Try it again." Her voice was rich and throaty, a warming purr. Hand away, she pulled her shoulder back, enthusiastically offering both her breasts.

Biting his tongue in concentration, he slid my switch, taking a long moment to adjust my vibration. Then, stroking my humming tip along the underside of each breast, he glanced back and forth from the sight of me sending undulations through her silken skin to her face for the tiniest flick of discomfort.

But she was certainly *not* uncomfortable. Arms flexing as I was touched to more or less sensitive areas, her breath quickened and her eyelids fluttered with quivers of pleasure.

"Okay," Rose said, fanning her fingers in front of her nipples in mock surrender.

"You like it?" Patrick said, holding me—still excitedly buzzing though not yet oscillating—off to the side.

"It's weird—but nice," Rose said. Thumbs into sides of panties, she slid them down. Sitting on the side of their bed she gently spread her legs. "Try it here."

Patrick's voice snagged in his throat. "Just a minute," he said, coughing between words. Putting me on the bed next to her, shoes were kicked aside, pants dropped, shirt pulled off and tossed into a corner, shorts following suit. Aroused, he leaned forward, kissed her as only new lovers can, grazing a hand across her breast and hardening nipple.

Breaking the kiss, she said "Come on, try it on me."

"You sure?" he said. Maybe because she was too excited by the prospect of enjoying me, she did not notice his tone—or that his erection dipped, wavered, and slightly sagged.

"Yeah, just a little at first." Leaning back, she displayed herself. "Right here." A finger at the top of her mons, pulling gently back, showing her deep purple hood and the red bead of her clitoris.

"Sure." Picking me up, he took even longer to adjust my settings. "No problem." Prudently he brought me down until my vibrating head was just above her and then down. Contact made.

Puckering up her mouth, she sang a long, simple melody of "oooohs" and slowly bucked the muscles of her ass in accompaniment. In response, her other lips puffed, moistened, spread. After a moment her eyes opened, after being shut in concentration, and she uttered a few real words: "Wow, that's nice. Try it all the way."

"Okay, if that's what you want." Down from her clit, gliding between those slippery lips, and—there—hovering at the entrance. "Ready?"

"Uh huh," she said, fully reclined, legs up and apart, excitement prominent.

In then—head first. Guided in with care, just enough force to part the inner ring muscles and, with a warm wet slide, within. Virgin no more, my own pleasure was as unmistakable as Rose's: a change in mechanical tempo mirroring her own escalating rate and shallowness of her breaths, flexing of her muscles. Mine in purpose fulfilled, hers in being filled by my Japanese-designed purpose.

Out then, and back in, and back out, a steady humming rhythm. Discovery, then Patrick mischievously slid one of my controls, and activated my band of pearls. Discovery, for her as well, as they acted against that sensitive area just an inch or so within her pussy, and Rose reacted with a deep, powerful moan of delight.

"Wait," she said after a stretched moment, pulling up from her obvious pleasure. "Try it like this." Hand down, she guided me in deeper, pushing until I was all the way in. "Do the ears now." Giggling, she drew her lips apart.

"You're the boss," he said, voice slow and deep. "Whatever you want."

Control box altered, my rabbit ears began their frantic fluttering, thin plastic buzzing between the valley of her upper lips, grazing the aroused tip of her clit. Control box altered again, he added twisting oscillations to my performance, and even deeper, even more throaty sounds to her orchestrations.

Pink vinyl within pinker depths, plastic vibrating along with her own excited movements; this was what I was made for. In being Rose's vibrator, I was as pleased—I believed at the time—as only she could be.

But even though I am a Rabbit Pearl Vibrator, manufactured in Japan, and retailing for approximately $90.00, and purchased in San Francisco at Good Vibrations, I was mistaken about something important.

Her orgasm was as delightful as it was loud and strong: legs stretched out and stiff, hands clutching clumps of bedspread. At first she hissed between tightly locked teeth, but then amplified to a soulful, bass bellow of ecstatic release. Coming, having come, and fading to gone, she fell back, body sheened with sweat, panting easing in volume and duration.

"Oh, wow," she said, giggles spilling out after the words. "That was intense."

"I'm glad," he said, turning me off and putting me aside.

"Are you sure?" Rose said, climbing up onto her elbows to look at him.

"Oh, yeah," he said, voice still low, deep, but also throaty with a different quality. "I was kind of nervous at first—that you'd like it too much, you know? But seeing you like that, man, it was such a turn on. I liked it, too. A lot."

Arms wrapped around him, she planted a flurry of kisses on his lips, cheeks, neck, and chest. "That's wonderful—I hoped you would. It was lots of fun, but only because you were on the other end of it." Sly grin on her glistening face, Rose added: "You know, there's a lot of other places we can try it—on you, as well as me."

"I'm game," Patrick said, sweet smile on his face. "Let's play."

Yes, I am Rabbit Pearl vibrator, who resides when not in use in a bedside table. I am certainly a tubular pink plastic device 5 inches long, 1-1/2 inches wide, and I was manufactured in Japan out of durable vinyl.

But I am not just Rose's vibrator. Instead I am a device used for the enhancement of sexual pleasure by both Rose as well as her boyfriend, Patrick—and they—and I—couldn't be happier.

SHADY WAYS
by Jocelyn Bringas

Tammy Crawford rolled her eyes when she saw her roommate, Rina St. John, and Rina's blond-haired boyfriend, Nick Laster, fooling around. She couldn't believe she had to endure them for her entire freshman year at college. Their giggles and kissing noises were really irritating as she tried to concentrate on writing a composition for her English class.

Her anger escalating, she slammed her binder shut, grabbed her toiletries bag, and stormed out of the dorm room. Walking down the corridor, she cringed when she heard moaning from nearly every direction. She hated being in McLanly Dorm, the horniest dorm on campus. Since she had enrolled late, she hadn't gotten the dorm she'd requested.

Erotic energy surrounded her. Was she the only person on campus not having sex? Still, from all the moaning she heard, she couldn't help but get aroused. She walked into the bathroom, found an empty shower stall, and turned on the water to let it warm up.

Once she'd undressed, she stepped inside the stall and relished the feeling of the hot water spraying down on her, easing her tense muscles. She lathered the soap into her hands and rubbed the bubbles all over her body, paying special attention to her nipples and the valley between her legs. As she caressed her full breasts, she threw her head back in pleasure, imagining it was Nick who was tweaking her nipples.

Even though the handsome blond was dating Rina, she couldn't help the nasty thoughts she had about him. His image flooded her mind as she slid her hand over her flat stomach, then slipped it between her legs and started to furiously rub her clit.

She let out a whimper as she imagined Nick thrusting his cock deep inside her. The familiar sensation of an orgasm struck her, and she started to grind her pussy harder onto her hand. Leaning back against the tiled shower wall, she softly moaned Nick's name as her clit seemed to burst in pleasure. She stayed in that position for a moment as she regained her breathing.

Painfully removing her fingers from her clit, she stood directly under the shower head before she turned off the water. She dried her body quickly, then slipped on her bathrobe and walked over to the sink.

The bathroom door opened and in walked Nick.

Damn coed bathrooms.

He smirked at her, and she focused her attention on the mirror. She hated him for being so handsome and having such bad taste in women. After brushing her teeth, she gathered her things and made her way out.

At least he was out of her and Rina's dorm room now. She could probably sleep in peace without having to endure Rina and Nick screwing like animals on the nearby twin bed. Her hand was on the doorknob to her room when a large hand covered hers. She turned to see Nick grinning mischievously at her.

"I thought you and Rina were done for the night," she said, quickly removing her hand from under his.

"Actually I'm here to see you. Calculus is murdering me and I know you happen to be the math whiz. So can you help me out on the homework?"

Tammy wanted to say 'no' and let him fail, but a nagging voice inside her head that made her say 'yes' instead.

"Cool," he grinned, "you're the best,"

She returned to opening the door but he stopped her again.

"Rina's sleeping. Let's go into my dorm. My roommate is at a frat party so it'll just be us."

"Let me change first," she said, finally opening the door. After changing into her sleeping attire, she grabbed her calculus notes and quietly left the room. Nick was waiting for her.

"This way," he gestured as he started to walk. Nick was a little bit ahead of her so she had a full view of his round butt that she had thought about numerous times. What she would give to have the opportunity to give it a nice spanking. After a few turns here and there, they arrived at his room. Walking in, she looked around and saw clutter everywhere. What irritated her most were the posters of nearly nude models plastered all over the walls.

"Excuse the mess," he said as he cleared his bed, then gestured for her to sit down. Wanting to get comfortable, Tammy sprawled out on her stomach with her notes in front of her. The bed was big enough for the two of them so Nick lay down next to her in the same position.

"I have no freaking idea how to do problem number five," he said pointing at it in the book.

As she examined the problem, she realized she had never been this close to Nick before. Copying the problem down onto her binder paper, she explained it thoroughly as Nick nodded.

"Do you understand?" she asked.

"It's getting clearer," he responded.

"Good, now let me see you do number six," she said as she yawned.

"Tired?" he asked as he copied number six down onto his paper.

"Mid-terms are killing me."

Tammy watched as he did the problem. She noted his decent handwriting and how he concentrated deeply on the calculus problem. "I'm not sure if it's right..." he said showing her his work. Looking at it, she smiled.

"You got it," she said handing his paper back to him. As he started the next problem, she turned onto her back and relaxed her neck. She glanced at Nick, wishing she could touch him.

"Thanks for your help," he said as he turned onto his back and got into the same position she was in.

"Uh huh," she said lazily not wanting to leave the comfort of his bed.

"Don't fall asleep." He punched her arm lightly.

"I better go," she said rolling back onto her stomach. As she closed the binder, she felt a hand on her waist. She slapped it away.

"What are you doing?"

"I was touching you," he said before he pressed his lips onto hers and kissed her. At first, she was in shock and didn't move. Nick kept fighting with her lips to kiss him back. The tip of his tongue outlined her lips and slowly her lips parted.   Tammy could feel the familiar tingle of arousal between her thighs as Nick pulled her closer. She tipped her head back, and Nick's lips were all over her neck. He moved his body to cover hers. She moaned as he nibbled the side of her neck, and for a second she almost forgot he had a girlfriend. A girlfriend who was her roommate. But once that thought crossed her mind, she pushed Nick away, making him fall down onto the cluttered floor.

"What the hell?" he muttered as he rubbed his head.

Embarrassed, she grabbed her binder and ran out. That probably was her only chance at having him. After running, she realized she was lost. She'd never been in this part of the dorm before. Had they walked through this common area on the way to his room? She couldn't remember. Sighing, she spotted a couch and sat down.

Tossing her binder to her side, she buried her head into her hands. She remained like that until she felt someone poking her shoulder. Lifting her head, she saw Nick dressed only in a pair of gray sweat pants. He took a seat next to her and she accidentally glanced at his crotch.

Nick had a hard-on and it was all her fault. Still, the fact that she was the cause of it excited her. Too bad she couldn't do anything about it. They sat in silence as the murmurs of sex flooded their ears. Tammy wondered how people could do it all night long; it seemed like a lot of excruciating work.

"I've seen the way you look at me," he said, tracing one hand along her thigh. "And I've been watching you, too."

"What about Rina?"

"What about her?"

She couldn't remember what about Rina. Not with Nick's hand

moving up her leg, higher and higher. Tammy moaned when she felt Nick's hand slide inside her pajama bottoms. Her head leaned back against the cushion as he softly massaged her through her panties. She arched her back as he rubbed her with his palm. Quickly, Nick pulled her pants and panties off her and spread her legs wide. He easily slipped two fingers inside her and started to move them in and out.

"You like that, baby," he whispered huskily as he pumped his fingers faster. Her response was a moan as she bucked her hips wildly against him. The feelings of pleasure built up inside her and she came all over his hand with her juices soaking his fingers.

"Sweet," he said after licking her juices off his fingers. He lifted her T-shirt next, and Tammy gripped his head as his tongue tickled her nipples. Cupping her breasts in each of his hands, he pushed them together as he swung his tongue from nipple to nipple. Nick stared at her intensely as he slowly circled the tip of his tongue around one of her hardened nipples. She found that intensely erotic.

He kissed his way down her body, and then placed her legs onto his broad shoulders as he dove his lips into her pussy.

"Oh, yes," she groaned as she felt his tongue circle around her drenched pussy. His hands held her hips as he lifted her up and licked her pussy. Tammy shuddered as she had another orgasm. She hadn't known a person could orgasm more than once in such a short amount of time.

Nick kicked out of his sweatpants before moving up next to her on the sofa and lazily nibbling her earlobe. She could feel his erection pressing against her thigh, so dangerously close to her pussy. Wrapping her arms around him, she raked her fingers down his back and right to his firm butt. She squeezed his skin and felt him grow harder.

"Damn, that feels good," he muttered.

After massaging his butt, she reached down and held his hardness. Nick was as hard as steel when she gripped him. Precome was already making Nick's cock glow and she could see the veins pulsing.

"That's it," he moaned as Tammy started to stroke him.

"Nick?"

"Yeah baby...,"

"I want to suck your cock," she said, and she felt Nick's cock twitch in her hands. Quickly, he moved into a kneeling position giving Tammy room to suck him.

"Yeah, suck it," he groaned holding her head in his hands as he fucked her mouth. It took a while for her to get accustomed to his length. He was so big and thick, but she did her best, sucking him until she felt him pull away from her.

"I need to fuck you, tell me you want me," Nick ordered as he pushed Tammy back down onto the couch. It was such a nice rush, especially being out in the open, where anyone could walk in anytime. But it was so late. What was the likelihood that they'd be caught?

"I want you, Nick," she moaned.

Nick grabbed her legs and placed them on his shoulders again with his stiff dick rested on her stomach as his balls brushed her clit.

"Please," she begged not being able to take it anymore.

Without warning, Nick inserted his full length into her and Tammy felt like she was being split apart. She moaned and whimpered as she felt him pump into her, and she squealed when Nick lifted her up and sat her with her chest pressed against his, still joined as one. His breath was coming in short gasps and his skin was shielded with sweat. He kissed her bare shoulder as he slowly moved himself inside her.

"Ride me, baby..." Nick whispered lying back down. Pressing her palms onto his chest, she lifted her hips and slammed back down. She liked the feeling of power she felt as she rode Nick's cock. It was empowering to have him writhing under her and grunting in pleasure.

Nick's hands were on her hips, guiding her as they moved in unison. *This is better than masturbating,* she thought as the surges of pleasure ran all over her body. She could feel it everywhere and not just at her core. Nick leaned his head up and tried to nibble on her jiggling nipples.

"Oh, god," she groaned as he added to her pleasure. She could feel the tingly sensation of an intense orgasm approaching. Nick was slamming into her so hard she could barely see what was in front of her, and she didn't protest at all when he flipped her around and took her doggy-style. She could only hear the slapping of skin to skin, and Nick's grunts.

Tammy felt herself drowning in a world pleasure. Her pussy started to contract around Nick's cock which sparked his orgasm. Nick thrust into her, until he was empty. She fell face down onto the couch as she tried to catch her breath.

"Oh my God!" a female voice yelled.

Tammy lifted her head up for one moment and through her faltered vision she saw Rina with her eyes widened in shock. She could feel Nick scrambling to get his pants on as he ran after her.

"I'm sorry, baby," Tammy heard him say to Rina as he went after her. Turning around, she grabbed her clothing and covered up her private parts. She felt tears sting her eyes as the reality that Nick would never love her back struck her. She was just something to do while Rina was sleeping.

Tammy felt a little dizzy while she tried to stand up. After putting on her clothes, she walked down the hall. When she turned the corner, her heart sank as she saw Nick passionately kissing Rina. She felt disgusted, but wasn't that payment for her own shady ways?

Turning around, she went back to the couch and cried herself to sleep.

TRYING IT FOR SIZE
by Saskia Walker

Shopping with James was, in itself, a stimulating activity. It was one of the many things that I adored about his company. That, and his tendency toward the extreme when it came to sex. I never knew what he'd suggest, nor when. It kept me on the edge of the most extraordinary sense of arousal and anticipation, because James could make even shopping for the mundane an adventure in discovery. Why, just the way he'd stand back in the market and watch me roll and squeeze a lemon in my hand, testing it for ripeness, made me feel dirty and bad, like he knew what I was thinking, even before I did.

When I saw him stalking into my office that Tuesday evening, something tripped inside me. He had *that* look on his face.

I was just closing my files for the day and he strode over to my desk, put his hands on its surface and leaned over to give me the briefest of kisses on the mouth. Passers-by on their way out of the building stared through the glass walls of my office in blatant curiosity. He had that effect on people. He was sexy as hell and oozed confidence. I looked up into his flashing green eyes. Anticipation raced in my blood. I stood up, walked round to him and ran my fingers through his spiky, blonde-tipped hair.

"Come on, hot legs, let's hit the town," he said, arresting me with one strong arm around my waist.

"I thought we were going to do that later." I'd agreed to help him select some new seating for his Cambridge web design studio.

"I decided that I like the way those eager little sales assistants look at you when you're dressed for business." He glanced down at my outfit. Yeah, so I dressed to provoke. Low cut, high on the thigh, heels you could pivot on. I enjoyed the powerful diva look. I also got way more business than all the other accountants on the floor. Hell, if you've got it, flaunt it, that's my motto.

James took me to a large office furniture outlet on the outskirts of the town. As he had predicted, an eager sales assistant popped up immediately when we strolled through the door. The lad was no more than 19 years old and the prospect of getting a sale so near the end of the day obviously pleased him. While he inquired after our needs, he gave me an appreciative once over, one hand tugging nervously at his slim-line tie, the other jangling the keys in his pocket. I glanced at James to see his reaction. A half smile played around his mouth; he rested his hands in the pockets of his elegant pants, looking on, completely unfazed.

"We're after some relaxed and comfortable office seating, something suitable for a customer reception area." The assistant nodded and directed us down through the large showroom, where matching sets of furnishings were grouped into different styles and materials.

"Just shout when you see something you like."

"How about that one," James said, nodding his head over to a Scandinavianlooking conglomeration, all smooth lines and interlocking pieces.

"Yes, that looks good," I agreed.

The assistant lurched off toward the mocked-up office. As we followed, James slid one hand down and squeezed my bottom through my skirt as we walked. I shot him an enquiring glance, but couldn't help smiling.

"This is an extremely popular and flexible design," the sales assistant commented, as he launched into a plethora of technical specifications and features worthy of the next NASA schedule. He began to move the furniture around, demonstrating how easily the chair units could be used, either butted up against one another or stand alone, and how the square inset units functioned as side tables or corner pieces to augment the chairs and turn them into a sofa. It was a practiced routine and his sales patter was award winning.

The footstool add-on had caught my eye. A simple, solid roll design on a sturdy plinth, and strong enough to use as a seat if necessary — so the sales assistant had commented as he shifted it into place in front of a chair. It was a smart and efficient accessory, well designed. In fact... it just looked as if it was begging to be tried out for versatility. As the thought permeated thorough my mind, I sensed that James was watching me. I glanced over. He flickered his eyebrows at me, suggestively. *Damn*..How did he always know when my mind wandered into the deviant zone?

That's when I suddenly remembered. In a rather wine-sozzled moment the week before, I had confessed to him that whenever I entered someone's home or workspace, I speculated over the erotic potential of their furnishings. Even a simple office chair could provoke the question as to what position it might be used in. Had James brought me here to the furniture store, on purpose, because of that?

As if in reply to my silent question, he suddenly grinned at me. I heard bells ringing; I felt like I'd been caught red-handed. What an absolute devil he was, setting me up like that! I managed to smile back, as nonchalantly as I could. That's when I realized the bell was a phone ringing, at the other end of the shop.

"I'm sorry, folks, I'm the only one here and I'm going to have to get that," the sales assistant said, and gave a reluctant shrug.

"Go ahead," replied James. "We can amuse ourselves while we wait." I knew that tone. What was he up to? The sales assistant hadn't noticed and was jogging off towards the front desk. As soon as he had picked up the phone, James hooked the toe of one polished boot around the leg of the footstool, and pulled it over towards him, so that it was stationed behind a tall cabinet and hidden from passers-by on the street.

"Why don't you try it," he suggested, nodding down at the item that had caught my attention.

"Try it?"

He put his head on one side, eyeing it up.

"It has to be about hip height... if you knelt." The surface of my skin raced with sensation, my body burning up with arousal. I swallowed. I couldn't quite believe it; he wanted me to try it out in the shop, now?

"I want to see you kneeling over it, that is what you were thinking wasn't it, you naughty girl?"

My imagining hadn't even got into that much detail, but now that he mentioned it... yes, it did look like the perfect playtime accessory.

"You know me so well, darling," I dared to reply, laughing nervously. I glanced down through the shop. The front door was still open but no one else had come in. The sales assistant was busy with his call. It sounded like a delivery problem. He was apologizing, big time, and trying to sort out a new time to suit the caller. *Well, it couldn't hurt just to try it out, could it?*

I knelt down on the floor where James had indicated, and rested my upper body right over the footstool. *Oh, yes.* It was just the right height. My hips were angled so that my pubis was squashed, my bottom pushed up and out behind me. It felt deliciously naughty.

"Very nice. Now pull your skirt up, so that I can look at that gorgeous derriere of yours."

I glanced back at him. *Surely he couldn't mean it? Not here, not in the shop.*

But I could see that he was already hard; his cock was bulging inside his pants. I looked up at his face and when I saw the look in his eyes, it triggered something inside me. *Yeah*, I decided, I wanted to show him all right. Right now. I reached back and shimmied the tight skirt up and over my hips, slowly revealing my buttocks and the black lace G-string I was wearing.

"Oh, yes," he murmured and his hand was moving against the front of his pants, up and down the length of his cock. My sex clenched. I wanted him there, badly. We would have to hurry home soon so that we could see this through.

I turned away and stared ahead to keep focused. I could just make out the pavement and cars racing past on the street outside, between the legs of the cabinet we were sheltered behind.

"We've got time, but it'll have to be quick, " James said, kneeling behind me and pulling my G-string down to my knees in one swift maneuver. I heard his zipper. *He couldn't be serious? Not the whole deal?*

"James —"

He chuckled low.

"It was your idea, lady. It was written all over your face, you horny little vixen."

"It wasn't... I mean, we can't, not here..." And then his hands were roving down the inside of my thighs and I was melting into submission.

I gasped when I felt the shaft of his erection hard between my thighs. He ran the swollen head back and forth between the folds of my sex, pushing me open and massaging my clit. I squirmed and whimpered, my fingers gripping at the legs of the stool. He increased the pressure and speed, one hand on my hip to steady himself. I began to shudder; the sensation was so intense. He continued the assault on my clit. My body arched; my hips bucked up. He pinned my body down with his hands on my shoulders.

"We can't do this," I whispered, pleading.

"We can," he replied. "We've got time, don't worry I'm listening out for him." With that, he eased the head of his cock inside me. My hips were angled to take him in, my flesh melting onto the hard, hot shaft.

"Christ, you're wet," he muttered. I hummed my pleasure aloud, my head falling back as my back arched. His hands were on my waist, pushing up my skirt and holding me locked into place over the stool. I suddenly caught sight of someone on the street pausing by the window, as if to come in. I couldn't bare the thought of having to stop now. No, this was too good to stop; I was so close to coming.

"Faster," I urged him, below my breath. "Please do it faster."

The figure moved on past the shop. I closed my eyes and rode the rhythm, thanking our lucky stars for giving us just another moment to enjoy this. James put one hand on the small of my back, and my clit was pressed right onto the surface of the stool; he rolled his hips forward, and drove home to the hilt. Sensation exploded through my groin.

"Hush, noisy girl." He reached forward with one hand and covered my mouth to keep me quiet. I blushed feverishly. He'd told me before that I sometimes raised the rafters when I came. I was oblivious to it under normal circumstances, but now we were doing it in public, in a shop of all places! I bit my lip, trying to quell the instinctive urge to give loud, vocal approval.

The containment of his hand on my mouth felt good; it felt deviant. He was thrusting hard and fast, deep inside me. My sex was on fire, my clit pounding from his earlier assault and the restless movement against the stool. My core was flooding, I was wired with tension. His fingers got tighter on my mouth as his cock arched inside me. I felt myself give and my sex suddenly spasmed in release. A stream of liquid heat ran down my thigh. James gave me one last feel of his length, his rigid cock roaring up inside me and jerking vigorously as he came.

I gasped when he freed my mouth, panting as I put my hands on the stool for balance and looked back at him. He grabbed my hair and held me while he kissed my mouth.

"Hurry, you've got about 10 seconds and you've lost a shoe," he commented.

I suddenly realized the distant voice on the phone had ended. James was standing up, I heard his zipper. I scrambled to my feet, dragging my G-string up and pulling my skirt into position. I managed to get my foot back in the shoe just as the sales assistant turned the corner.

"I'm so sorry to have kept you..."

His voice trailed off as he caught sight of me straightening my skirt. I smiled at him and did up the button on my shirt that had popped open.

"No problem, we were enjoying ourselves," James replied.

The sales assistant looked from one of us to the other. I felt my cheeks burning. James grinned, and then winked at the poor lad, who was clearly wondering what he had missed. I glanced away and tried to ignore the trickle of liquid running down the inside of my thighs.

"I'll phone through the rest of my order tomorrow, but we'd like to take this item with us now." James said, as he handed over his credit card and scooped up the footstool under his arm. "We were trying this one for size," he had the cheek to add. "And I have to say..." He winked at me. "It fits real good."

UNLEASHED
by Sage Vivant

Of all the toys and all the playgrounds available to him that morning, Boyd chose the sauna in which to begin his week of house sitting.

Sweating made him feel cleansed and oddly relaxed. And it was the only time when a blurry atmosphere was what he was supposed to be seeing, not what his glasses were made to correct.

So, as he waited for Jocelyn in the house the Coopers had so graciously asked him to watch while they traveled, he surrendered his overworked body to the steamy warmth that filled the sauna. He wanted to be at his best when she arrived. This trip, he would show her that he was ready for anything—any wild escapade, any exhibitionist undertaking, and all manner of sexual indulgences. He couldn't really imagine, after sex on the beach in Bermuda and then in the mountains of Washington, that she could shock him with any new challenge when she came to Florida. Nevertheless, she was always full of surprises, and he didn't intend to disappoint her by being mentally unprepared for anything.

As the heat started to tickle his perspiring skin—the first sign that he needed to think about getting out soon—he tried to imagine just what she might ask of him this time that would surprise him. Though he came up with very little, he developed an instant hard-on that he would loved to have shown her had she been there. *Soon*, he thought eagerly. *Soon*. In the meantime, thinking about her too much before she arrived was clearly not a good way to refresh himself, so he concentrated on some details he'd just learned about one of the projects he was due to begin at the non-profit he worked for in Atlanta. Shortly thereafter, the heat in the sauna became oppressively brutal, so he darted out and into the cool, tiled anteroom to bring down his body temperature.

He showered and donned only his swim trunks before heading for the pool. He practiced his swagger on the way, pretending that the gorgeous estate was his own and that he'd known such luxury all his life. A smooth confidence powered his stride and fueled the smile on his face until he arrived at the pool where, to his delighted alarm, Jocelyn lay naked on a chaise, with only sunglasses to protect her from potential sun damage. Her dark skin soaked up rays as if she had been raised in the tropics.

He felt the swagger dwindle and fade as desire replaced it. His attraction to her fired him with youthful exuberance and renewed sexual energy that he hadn't known for many years. As he watched her now, he struggled between sneaking up and surprising her with some clever greeting or staring at her until she felt his need and came to him with a delicious way to fulfill it.

As it happened, she saw him while he was in the throes of this deliberation.

"Hey, sexy! I hope you don't mind that I made myself at home."

She propped herself up on her elbows, which gave him a better view of her perky little breasts. It was hard to miss those tantalizing nipples even from several feet away. He recovered himself quickly and approached her with his most casual attitude.

"Not at all," he replied. "I'm glad you're here. Whatever it takes to make you comfortable is fine by me." That her comfort usually required her nudity was just an added bonus.

He sat on the edge of the chaise next to her. The instant he saw her, he'd gotten hard and now that erection tented his swim trunks to an extent that seemed futile to try disguising.

"I see you *are* glad to see me," she purred, removing her sunglasses. Her attention to his bulge made it bigger. He was both mortified and proud of his cock's enthusiasm. What it needed soon, though, was release. He had never been comfortable asking for that, but with Jocelyn, it didn't matter—she knew what he wanted and she was ready to provide it. He laughed nervously.

"Don't I get a kiss?" She smiled, chuckling good-naturedly at his discomfiture.

He leaned forward to reach her face. "I'm so sorry, sweetheart. With all that gorgeous flesh in front of me, I must have forgotten my manners."

Their lips met in a long, slow, getting-to-know-you-again kiss.

"Hi," she whispered. Her brown eyes penetrated his with genuine affection. He felt himself beginning to melt.

"How long have you been here?"

"Maybe twenty minutes. My luggage is over there." She nodded toward the gate where she'd entered. Her traveling clothes were draped over her suitcase, indicating that she'd sauntered along the length of the pool to the chaise wearing nothing. He wondered briefly if the Coopers ever sunbathed naked, and if so, if they ever worried about offending the neighbors.

She laughed, reading his mind, or rather, his insecurities. "Don't worry. Nobody can see us. This place is so private, it might as well have its own zip code."

"Oh, I'm not worried," he assured her. "I thought I'd take a swim. Would you like to join me?" He was still somewhat warm from the sauna and the noonday sun wasn't helping.

"Absolutely. Last one in has to take an early flight home."

The joy of watching her scamper toward the pool's edge and leap in like a happy child was worth being the last one in. He followed her, jumping in only seconds after she did. They splashed and played, squealing and chasing, laughing and calling out to each other. What he referred to as her "mermaid side" was in top form—she swam around the pool with graceful speed, weaving reckless paths through the chlorinated water. She snaked unpredictably near his legs, sometimes swimming between them when his stance was wide enough. He knew she did it to torment him, that he would wonder what she was up to, and she was right. He wanted her to stop but feared that she would. Finally, just when he resigned himself to thinking she was only doing her Esther Williams impression, she dallied between his legs and with one decisive yank, pulled his trunks down to his knees.

He laughed and dog-paddled frantically. With his cock so stiff, there was no telling how it would respond to anything she might have in mind for it. With another tug at his trunks, they slid down the length of his legs. She rose to the surface, whirling the waistband around her finger in victory.

"Doesn't that feel better?" Those dark eyes sparkled with mischief as droplets of water glistened on her skin.

"Well, sure, but—"

"But nothing! You're about to feel even better." She dove underwater again and headed straight for his crotch. Instinctively, he spread his legs, uncertain where she'd focus her attention but content with whatever she decided. Though his tip ached for her touch, she honed in on the small spot between his swollen balls and his asshole. She fingered him there, causing his back to arch and his breath to grow shallow. With her other hand, she played cautiously at his asshole until his cock threatened to burst from anticipation.

She came up for air in one big expulsion from between his legs. "How's that?"

He forced himself to recall the part of his brain that permitted speech. "Oh, god, it's good," he blurted. He hoped she wasn't finished.

She wasn't. Swooping back down again, she grabbed his member and pumped it. With her free hand, she cupped and squeezed his balls, which were now so tight and close to his body, he felt he could come with just a command. She rubbed and stroked, rubbed and stroked—until she came up for air again.

"I'd say you're ready for some serious fucking," Jocelyn cooed as she wrapped her arms around his neck and steered him toward the pool's edge.

"That's all I've been thinking about for weeks," he confessed.

Holding his thickness with one expert hand, she used her buoyancy to straddle and mount him. Even in the water, her pussy was unmistakably wet and warm. Once he was inside her, a shiver started at his toes and shot up through his body. "You feel so good," he gasped.

"You do, too." Her mouth was immediately on his, and her closeness made him dizzy with unfocused, unbridled lust.

With the soles of her feet behind him and against the side of the pool, she rode his grateful cock with the ethereal, sweeping motions possible only underwater. Her lovely breasts floated in exquisite tandem with the rise and fall of her body. He wasn't sure how much longer he could control himself. She continued to kiss him as she rode him until the point at which both of them stiffened, prepared for the imminent explosion. Without comment, she slid up and off him.

"What's wrong?" he asked, stunned and unspeakably horny.

"I need you to take me from behind," she explained, leading him by the cock to the stepladder out of the pool.

She led him to the chaise where a towel was draped over an arm. In one uninterrupted motion, she spread the towel on the patch of grass nearby and got on all fours. He forgot to breathe as he took in her dark, shapely, upturned ass, watching as it practically wagged its invitation for him to fuck it. She ran one hand along the curve of one ass cheek.

"Come on, Boyd. Put that beautiful cock in me."

A southern gentleman never disappoints a lady—wisdom that served him well at this moment. He didn't have to think about getting on his knees behind her, spreading those luscious cheeks wide, getting a good look at her waiting pussy and swollen lips, and then thrusting into her hot sweetness. In only a few strokes, he let loose months' worth of bottled up desire.

She threw her head back and moaned her own gratitude, spasming around his cock in a battery of super-charged pulses of joy. She slammed her ass into his cock to take him deeper and deeper.

When it was over, they lolled about in the grass, too exhausted even to cool off in the pool.

The lazy but sexually charged days passed all too quickly. Between "69" sessions on the banquet table, experiments with bondage on the four-poster bed, and all manner of oral sex in the most conspicuous of places, Boyd felt he was getting more out of the house than the Coopers ever could have.

Jocelyn, an accomplished sailor, wanted to take the sailboat out for a spin on day four of their vacation. Boyd had sailed with her before and had no qualms about entrusting her with his friends' boat. So, after a leisurely breakfast, they made their way to the dock and set sail for a lovely foray into the clear waters of the Emerald Coast.

"I really ought to learn how to sail," Boyd commented as Jocelyn masterfully maneuvered the craft into the gulf.

"Would you like to learn today?"

Actually wouldn't, but it was too late to rescind his comment. "Sure," he said, hoping she'd hear the reluctance in his voice and postpone the lesson.

"The first thing you have to learn is that your captain is all-knowing and allpowerful," she said, donning the captain's hat she'd found in the aft deck. She looked devastatingly adorable— not to mention incredibly fuckable.

"No problem there," he replied.

"And anything she asks has to be strictly obeyed. No back talk."

"Yes, ma'am."

"Excellent, matey. Rub some oil on your captain, then."

His heart leapt. These were the kinds of lessons he could enjoy.

She'd rigged the sails so the calm winds would just keep the boat serenely afloat. Without a shred of modesty, she removed her bikini top and handed him a bottle of suntan oil.

Instinctively, he looked around to make sure other sea faring vessels weren't enjoying the same view of her lovely nakedness that he was.

She laughed at his caution. "Don't worry. Once you start working on me, we'll be too low in the boat for anybody to see us."

She was right, as usual. He took the bottle from her. Just before he complied with her request, though, he found himself consumed by the desire to suck at her tits. He knew he'd be unable to focus on anything else until he got her pretty, plump nipples them between his lips. He leaned into her left breast and commenced to sucking, savoring the swollen nipple and licking it to see just how hard it could get. He kneaded the other breast in his free hand, eventually switching his mouth to that side while he rolled the other nipple between his fingers. Her moans told him he was pleasing his captain.

"Don't forget the oil," she reminded him after several minutes.

Dutifully, he poured some oil into his hands. As he rubbed it between his palms to ready it for application, she leaned back, spread her legs, and shot him the most challenging "come hither" look he'd ever seen. "You can rub that wherever you think you should," she purred. "I'll leave the decision to you."

He spread the oil in slow, sensuous arcs over her arms, shoulders, breasts, tummy, thighs, and calves. No part of her was off limits. He removed her bikini bottom to smooth the oil over her exquisite ass. He rolled her over gently to reach a breast, then the inside of a thigh or the small of her back. Every inch of her thrilled him, and as he treated himself to the feast that was her body, his cock stood at unwavering attention.

"Your captain now needs to suck the first mate's cock," she said, as officiously as her arousal would allow.

She'd told him once that sucking him stretched her mouth in new ways because he was so thick. He would forever think of that remark whenever she deepthroated him. Her tongue whipped circles around his cock, from the base to the tip, while she sucked him. He liked the way she closed her eyes when she attended to his dick, like she was lost in some heady erotic dream. Periodically, though, she'd look up at him with seductively playful eyes, leaving him with a whole new wave of need.

His knees were weakening now as her relentless mouth had its way with him. She looked up and saw the helpless expression on his face, then pulled back.

"Your captain has another request."

"I am at your service."

"I want you to be the ship's masthead."

Oh no. What was she up to?

When he didn't respond, she explained her request in detail. "I want you to strip naked and stand on the foredeck like a lookout. I want your beautiful cock to guide this boat."

He tried to laugh off her command, hoping she'd see how ludicrous it was to expect him to expose himself to oncoming vessels.

"Begging the captain's pardon, but how will that exercise teach me to sail?"

"Do I hear insubordination? One more word from you, matey, and I will have to consider your refusal to carry out orders outright mutiny!"

Strangely, his cock was still hard. He looked down at it and then at her. Her face softened a bit before she spoke again.

"I don't know why you hesitate. Most men would love to have a piece like yours. You should be proud to show it off. Besides, it would make me so hot if you stood there showing your cock to the world. I'll give you a special treat if you obey."

His primary consolation, as he made his way to the foredeck, was that there were very few boats out that day and that those that were out were far enough away to see nothing of what was about to transpire on the Coopers' boat.

With an erection that suddenly did seem large enough to guide any craft through safe or unsafe waters, he held on to the mast and stood tall. He imagined himself as one of those proud Viking figures, affixed to the bow of a boat with an air of majesty and courage. The sea spray tickled his hard-on but he continued to pose as instructed, torn between stifling hysterical laughter and wondering how Jocelyn might be planning to reward him for his fine seamanship.

He heard her squeal with delight just before she stationed herself at his crotch and finished the blow job she'd started earlier. As she sucked him, she played with her pussy—his exposure seemed to turn her on as much as it excited him. As he slowly surrendered to her hungry sucking, he gripped the mast and held tight. She surprised him by releasing him midway through his spurt, allowing his stream to flow from him like water from a fountain. And so he stood on the bow, shooting his pleasure into the Gulf of Mexico, standing proudly as the boat's masthead.

When he was finished, and completely spent by the high seas adventure she'd just concocted for him, she helped him back to the cockpit, where she soothed his overworked, oversexed body with a massage. Though he never learned how to sail that day, he certainly developed a finer appreciation for the versatility of sailboats.

The remaining two days of their glorious vacation were indescribably wonderful, but not quite so memorable as his sailing lesson. He'd not shirked from anything she wanted to do that week, and he felt more expansive, more alive, than at any time in his life. Jocelyn was so good for him. But she was a hell of a task mistress when it came to sailing.

VICKY AT THE VILLAROSA
by Bill Noble

Vic wasn't the sort of woman you said no to.

"Sunday at ten, right?"

"You bet!" he said brightly, hoping she couldn't hear his heart hammering over the phone. Maybe they were *too* perfectly matched: he'd never met a woman with such a ferocious libido. For weeks they'd upped the ante every time they'd met or talked, intensifying every encounter, going all out. It had become a contest.

"Well?" she said.

"Well what?" he answered, knowing exactly what she meant.

"What do you want to do?"

He shifted his straining cock to a more comfortable position. "Brunch?" he asked, knowing evasion wouldn't buy him any time.

"*Bill.*"

"Okay, okay. Wear that flowered dress. The silk one?" He tried to breathe deeply. "And no panties." He imagined his hand ghosting up the silk skin of her thigh, all the way to the hip, all the way to the constriction of the belt across her smooth belly. His fingers tingled with her heat. Possibilities started building in his head, replacing his apprehension.

"That's better," she said. "What else?"

"You . . . you really will do anything I say?"

She was silent, waiting him out. He knew the grin: her mouth in a wry tilt, her pale eyes dancing.

He spoke. "You know that little café in the courtyard on

Magnolia? The Villarosa? The one with the tablecloths that drape right to the floor?" His hand was shaking as he brushed hair back from his forehead.

She stayed silent, but he heard her breath quicken.

"So . . . get there just at ten. You won't be late?"

Silence. She wasn't going to help him out.

"Sit at the back table, in the little alcove that looks out over the marsh." His words were starting to come in a rush now, and his cock ached. "Get crepes—lingonberry crepes. Two orders. And some really dry white wine. And when I come in, when I'm still by the door, you know, when the waitress is looking in my direction . . . slip under the table." He gulped for air.

"A blow job," she breathed. Her voice had dropped half an octave.

"Hardly," he said. *God, am I really sure I want to set this up? I know she's brave enough to do it.*

"Then what?" A tremor of alarm.

"Vic," he said. "Lick your finger." He'd gotten the edge over her now. He could feel it.

"Under the table?"

"No, right now."

"I'm in my office. Felicia's right across from me." She was whispering into the phone.

"Well, we could always put it off a week."

Another long silence, but this one with a different flavor. "Okay," she said. He could tell she'd slipped a hand between her legs, just from the wobbly way the two syllables came out.

"Touch yourself," he said, running his nails the length of his cock. "And no, not a blow job. You're going to fuck me. Fuck me, right under the table."

"No way." He thought he could catch the tiny sounds of her wetness behind the jump of fright.

"Oh, yes," he told her, feeling more in charge every minute. "I'll slide forward on the seat, as if I were going to kneel on the floor. You raise your ass up and back into me. You're wet already."

"Ah," she said. He could barely hear her. "Under the table?"

"Under the table and right now. But there, I'll thrust my cock into you and smile at the waitress. I bet we'll get the freckled one. You know, the one with the wide hips you always lust after? She'll smile back at me as she serves sausages and pancakes to the next table. Know why?"

"Uh-huh." A whisper.

"Tell me."

"She'll know precisely what we're doing." Vicky was the one struggling to breathe now. The last word trailed away, out of breath.

"You'll be doing all the moving," he said. "While I'll hold perfectly still, to make sure you don't knock the dishes off the table." A pause, "Are you getting ready to come?"

"Uh, under the table?"

It was his turn to play silent.

"Yes," she said. "I am," she pled, in the tiniest voice. Each sharp breath ended in a mew that only the two of them could hear. He sensed her wetness more distinctly, heard the pace of her fingers.

"But there's one thing you need to know." His cock was out and he was pumping in time with her finger.

"Aah?"

"Sunday, when you get right to the edge of coming?"

"Yes?"

"I'll pull out."

She took three stuttering, harsh breaths without letting any air out.

"And you'll turn around and tuck me back in my pants, and then sit back up at the table. Like nothing happened."

A long, high, suppressed sound came out of the phone. He heard her teeth clack hard against the receiver as she almost dropped the phone. A distant voice said *Vic, are you okay?* He imagined—no, he *felt*—her pussy clamp down. His vision went black as his seed spurted into his hand, pulse after pulse, emptying him.

Their breathing rasped in and out of sync as they came down from it. His cock, slippery and spent, rested on the heel of his hand. His come spilled between his fingers, spattering the floor.

"I'm fine," he heard Vicky say to someone, "just something

caught in my throat." She didn't sound as if she expected anyone to believe her. "Bill?" She whispered into the phone.

"Yeah?" All the power he'd summoned was leaking away, but he didn't care.

"Lick it out of your hand!" she whispered. "Taste it! It tastes like both of us."

He raised his cupped, shaking hand to his mouth. He did. It did.

Sunday was only two days away.

WHEN THE CAT'S AWAY
by Trisha Dillon

It shouldn't matter whether he's in town or not, right? Shouldn't matter if he's across town at his upscale Penthouse apartment or across the country at a highend hotel. I should be true to him regardless of his physical location. I know that. At least, the good-girl part of me does. But when he's gone, something strange happens to both me and my morals. When I take him to the airport, drop him off, and then return to my car, I'm a changed being.

I sit there in the parking lot, redoing the makeup lining my eyes, using the heavy dark pencil that he thinks looks slutty. And you know what? It *does* look slutty, but that's okay. Slutty can be good sometimes.

Slutty can be perfect.

As I drive toward home, I unbutton the front of my pale blue shirt, so that the little peach lace camisole peeks through. I know right where I'm going. The car seems to know, as well, maneuvering easily through L.A. traffic to my favorite bar on Main Street. Before I get out of my convertible, I spritz on my chosen perfume for the evening. He doesn't like this one. Too musky, he says. And you know what? He's right. But the scent suits this side of me. The side that hikes up my short black silk skirt to make it even shorter right before I get to the door, the side that banters easily with the bartender, throwing out jokes as if I'm a stand-up, comfortable in my environment.

The drink is waiting for me before I get to the far stool in the corner. When I'm with *him*, I drink chilled white wine. One glass an evening. The expensive stuff that never gives you a headache. When I'm on my own, I prefer tropical drinks made with rum. The flirty pastel-colored drinks that always come with a stick of pineapple and neon-red cherries in a row. I lick my lips after the first sip, and the bartender gives me an approving wink. Joe likes what he sees, I can tell. Would he like more?

I don't have to ask.

I simply nod my head toward the back room and he meets me there seconds later. I'm wet already at the thought of what we're going to do. I've been wet since I exited the airport. Probably since *he* told me that he would be out of town this weekend. Can't explain why—that's just how it is with me. When he's away, my libido rages out of control. Everything is about wants and needs. *My* wants and needs. All other feelings pale next to the rush of lust that pulses through me.

Joe's hands are rougher and larger than his. They lift me up on the desk in the back office and spread me out easily. I'm ready for him. My short black skirt comes up naturally, and just as naturally Joe pops the fly of his faded jeans and lets me get a look at his hard-on. I lean up to grip it, more comfortable man-handling a rock-hard cock than I am at any other time. I know how to pump my fist, how to jack Joe's cock until he groans and tells me, "Now."

Now. I like the sound of that.

When I slip back onto the desk again, he slides inside of me. His fingers search out my small breasts, pushing the camisole aside and firmly pinching my nipples between thumb and forefinger. My nipples harden, and I moan out loud. With my man, I never moan. I'm silent as our bodies move together. I close my eyes and breathe in sweet and low. I never make any noise at all. Don't know why. Can't explain it. That's just how it is when we're together. It's how it always is, how it always will be.

As Joe fucks me, I can hear the music from the jukebox in the other room. I hear patrons laughing and growing rowdy. I think about the kind of girl who would fuck her bartender during working hours. The kind of girl who could then smooth her skirt and go take her seat back at the barstool, knowing that wetness is slicking her inner thighs as she leans forward to sip from her frothy rum drink.

Thoughts like these create an instant pleasure that spirals through me. I gaze up at my handsome barman and I see in his dark blue eyes that Joe thinks I'm sexy. So sexy. *Too* sexy.

And you know what? I am.

At least, when the cat's away.

X-POSE
by Lina Pierce

There are defining moments in all of our lives. Mine came tonight in the form of a man. I had been invited to a cocktail party by my friend, June. When she called me up, she had to convince me to go.

"Lily, I know these events can be such a bore, but I promised my boss that I'd have some of his business associates over, and they're supposed to be an interesting group of people. Who knows? You might have a good time. You might even meet someone."

I resisted and she insisted and finally as a favor to her I said yes.

It's not that I don't enjoy people. I just prefer really close relationships. The rest of my time is preoccupied with my career as a clothing designer or spent reading or working out at the gym. I don't spend too much time making small talk with strangers if it's avoidable. Yet I had promised June so I rose to the occasion. If nothing else, it was a good excuse to wear some outrageous outfit.

No matter what, I always wear great underclothes. Not for other people. For myself. Tonight, I decided to go classic. Pearls. Black lace evening dress. Black spike heels. Black silk stockings that hugged tight to my sleek thighs. The dress was subtlety transparent and I knew that I could go au natural or pick some perfect nude silk bra and thong panties to give the illusion of nakedness. Being both a little wild and a little reserved, I chose the magic of illusion.

June greeted me at the door, handed me a martini, and simply said, "Mingle." I found myself alone in a mix of guests, all talking and power cruising. And then, I saw this man in the crowd. He was by himself but seemed extraordinarily comfortable, both self-assured and self-contained. Although he was good looking, my attraction to him went beyond the physical. I felt compelled to talk with him but by the time I reached his side of the room, some other femme fatale had nabbed his attention, and I was forced to talk stock market with some nice but dreary soul.

The evening wore on and I lost track of the man, but to my happiness he ha not lost track of me. Almost magically he appeared by my side, introducing himself. "I'm Michael," he said, extending his hand. "And what can I do for you—?" he paused for me to fill in my name.

I laughed a little at his opening line. "I'm Lily. And I'm not so sure you can do anything for me." Instead of responding, he arched his eyebrow and let it go at that. I didn't know why I already felt drawn to this man, but I was determined not to let him know.

When it was clear no elaboration was forthcoming, I turned to walk away, secretly wondering what he meant by his question and hoping that he was going to stop me from leaving. No such luck. Irritated with myself and in no mood to socialize further, I retreated upstairs to June's sitting room.

The quiet room was decorated in rich woods, and the light from the marble fireplace created a warm inviting glow. I settled into a plush burgundy velvet couch. Staring into the flickering flames, I watched as their colors and shapes changed, so mesmerized that I didn't immediately realize when someone else wandered into the room.

Michael didn't ask whether he could join me. He simply made himself comfortable on the couch at my side. My heart pounded fiercely, but I managed what I hoped was an engaging smile. Now if I could only think of something witty or enticing to say. I could barely believe my own ears when I asked him, "So what are you really passionate about in your life?" Not exactly in the league of

"And what do you do?" but frankly on some level I didn't even care. I just wanted to get to know him and wanted him to know me.

My question appeared to please him. He smiled slightly, looked me in the eyes and without hesitation said just one word, "Intimacy."

His response inspired me to probe further. "Oh really?" I dared. "Then let's get intimate right now."

He waited patiently for me to continue.

"What's the wildest thing you've ever done?" I challenged him.

Michael laughed knowingly. "Maybe you asked me that because you have wild things on your mind."

"Au contraire," I retorted, perhaps a little too quickly.

He looked into my eyes again and said, "Maybe, maybe not, but this is what I have to offer you," he paused for a beat, "Freedom."

I could feel myself getting self righteous. "You can't offer me that. I'm already free."

"Okay," he said agreeably.

Now I was confused. "What exactly are you talking about?"

"It's simple. I don't judge you. You don't judge me. Be anyway you want with me."

My head swam. I still didn't know exactly what he was alluding to, but I was extremely intrigued.

"Do you trust me?" he asked, "Or, rather, do you want to trust me?"

"I'd like to trust you," I admitted

He lightly put his hand on mine. I felt his touch — electric. "Then, know there is nothing you can do or say that will alienate me. Forget about the past. What's the wildest thing you can imagine doing right now?"

Something in his words and his way just clicked. I considered the possibilities and made a quick decision. Standing in front of the fireplace, I looked him in the eyes and ever so slowly started raising the hem of my cocktail dress. As the dress glided up past my stockings and uncovered bare upper thighs, I realized I must decide how far I was willing to go. Michael was looking at me, intrigued and detached at the same time. His expression compelled me further.

I raised the hem just above the peek of my panties, then spread my legs apart and just stood there for a moment. My heart was beating really fast. I held the dress up with one hand and with the other I pulled the panties aside to reveal my pussy. I wondered how much Michael could see. The room was dimly lit and the fire, back lighting me, gave off a golden glow. Michael remained composed, but I could tell that he was drinking me in like a parched desert wanderer imbibing fresh water. I knew it was more than what he could see. For somehow unknowingly, I was finding a way to rock his world. And that really turned me on.

I slid the panties off, then raised my dress again. Posing there, utterly exposed, exceptionally naked in this state of semi-undress, I experienced a wonderful sense of vulnerability and power. I was a wickedly bad girl while simultaneously being remarkably washed clean. Thus liberated, I placed my index finger up to my mouth and slowly slipped the tip of my tongue out to touch my finger. Then I sucked my finger deep into my mouth and got it nice and wet. Still watching him, I took that finger and rubbed my clit. Spreading my lips apart, I pushed my finger deep inside, then pulled it out slowly. I walked back to Michael and positioned myself at his feet. I brought my finger to his lips and traced the outline of his mouth, feeling his breath on my hands. At first, I wasn't sure how he would respond, and that scared me and excited me even more. Then his tongue met the tip of my finger, licked and then sucked my finger, rich with wetness, into his mouth.

After releasing my finger from his mouth, he stopped for some wonderfully long seconds and stared right into my eyes as I remained by his feet. As he lifted his hands, I was convinced he would unzip his pants but instead he slowly started to loosen his tie. Ever so fastidiously he unbuttoned his white shirt, one button at a time, as I watched, entranced. When his shirt was mostly open, he took my hand and placed it, palm open, over his heart and he resolutely kept my hand pinned tight against him with his open hand. I felt the softness of his skin, the heat of his body, his chest pressed against my palm and then the steady strong beat of his heart. This vibration filled my whole body and it seemed as if the world had stopped and that the only reality that existed was Michael and I. And without thought, I experienced an overwhelming rush of love. This man was rocking my world like no one ever had.

And by his simple act, I chose to make the next move. Not because he wanted me to or because he asked but because I longed to. Kneeling, I rubbed my hand between his legs and felt the shape of his penis pressing against his pants. I took my time, exploring. My fingers searched the contours of this wonderful discovery until I could wait no longer.

After carefully unbuckling his leather belt, I unzipped his pants. His cock reached up to meet my hand. I d felt its warmth, magic hardness around the girth and wonderful softness at its tip. Suddenly, all I wanted to do was take Michael's cock into my mouth and suck. But first I let his hardness fill the palm of my hand as I introduced my tongue to the head. Michael took a deep breath of obvious pleasure. I slowly ran my tongue around the rim and then up and down his shaft. My warm breath played on his skin. I could feel Michael slowly surrender to me. Together we pushed his pants down. He spread his legs and I licked his balls and stroked his penis in my hand. I took in the heat and his own unique scent, all inviting me to continue. His hand gently touched my hair.

I made an O with my lips and first let the tip slowly come into my mouth. I sucked lightly, feeling the shape with my tongue, luxuriating in the sensation. And then ever so slowly, my lips firm around his cock, I let in more of him until I reached the base. And ever so slowly I retraced my steps until I was back at his tip. As Michael's breathing sped up, so did my motion, until finally I was sucking hard and moving fast. Michael now joined me as he rocked his hips and plunged his cock deeper into my mouth. Our counter motions created a perfect dance and I could feel the subtle changes in his body letting me know that he was close to coming. I focused my lips especially on his head as he rode into me. I felt the driving force of this man yet at the same time, he maintained a gentle consciousness of me. Then as I let him far into my mouth he climaxed with a perfect moan, releasing all his warm come into my mouth. The milky smoothness filled my mouth and then I swallowed as his being became a part of me.

Somewhat breathless, we filled our lungs with the wood-burnt air. Michael cupped his hands around my face and drew me up so I was sitting on his lap. He brought my lips to his. His breath mingled with mine and I melted into his body.

Gazing into each other's eyes, I caressed his face. I touched his forehead and nose and traced the tips of fingers against his freshly shaven cheeks. I ran my fingers through his cropped hair. Then I stopped and he touched my face with such tenderness that I almost cried. Our lips met and then our tongues until our mouths were firmly pressed against each other. I was lost in this world and I never want to return.

Then I heard noises at the door and remembered where we are, and we both hurried to compose ourselves. I slid on my panties as he zipped up his pants as the door opened, and June and some other guests joined us in the room. Our privacy had been utterly shattered. Secretly I yearned for more. But I knew that I must put back on my party persona and both Michael and I greeted our invaders graciously.

"Lily," June chided sweetly. "I've been wondering where you've been."

I slipped into my best Mona Lisa smile and innocently added. "Oh up here, getting to know Michael."

Now the night did not end in some fairy tale where I rode off into the early dawn with Michael. He did walk me to my car. He did not tell me it was the most incredible night of his life or that he couldn't wait to see me. And with his seeming reticence, I too held back. As I sat behind the driver's wheel, he leaned over and whispered in my ear just one word. "Again?"

I looked at him and I said, "Yes, again."

And as I drove away, I whispered to myself. "Again and again."

YOUR OLD SHIRT
by Gwen Masters

I am wearing your old shirt. To a casual observer that wouldn't be a very big deal, but it is to me. Your shirt is old and faded and worn, with little threads peeking out from their hiding places and colors beginning to bleed into the white parts. It smells like you most of the time, and it sometimes smells like my vanilla, sometimes it just smells like soap from my washer. But it is comfortable, it is yours, and by extension, mine.

I wear this shirt a lot. I wear it when I need to feel sexy, which is pretty often lately, I admit. I feel that way right now. It is late in the evening and you are sound asleep, in some distant city and an unfamiliar bed, resting after another long day of chasing a dream for us. I wandered this house alone tonight and spent quite a while just looking at the candles burning on my table, thinking about us.

But I don't want to think anymore. I just want to feel you.

I want to feel you in front of me, knowing your eyes are devouring me, knowing that you can see everything under this shirt with your mind. I want to feel your hands reach out and slowly push a curl of wayward chestnut hair back behind my ear, letting your fingers trail down the soft strands until you find the even more enticing softness of my neck. I want to shiver while you run your fingertips over my skin and feel the pulse beating underneath the softness. I know you. I know you would do this, because you don't know how not to worship a woman.

You might say things, or you might not. It wouldn't matter because I know what is in your heart at times like this, during long nights like these. Your heart would proclaim that I am beautiful and I would, finally, at long last believe...you would tell me that I am the only one you want, and this I would no longer doubt. Your hands would delve into my hair and you would pull my head back, and I would enjoy the long moment of just our breath mingling before you kissed me. And you would kiss me the way a woman deserves to be kissed, with a tender touch and a demanding hand, all at once. The passionate side of you that needs control would make itself known. And I would answer with a moan, a motion of assent.

I want you. I would say that somehow, although maybe not in words. But you would already know it, because you would already feel the heat within my skin, see the darkness in my eyes. I want you. I want you to touch me. I want to feel like myself, like yours, again. My fantasy goes farther. Do you want to know?

In my mind, my fantasy, you pull my head back just enough to slide your soft lips down my throat. You find that little hollow and suck gently, making me smile because I know you are very cautiously leaving a mark there. You don't know what I want yet and you are testing the waters. But you are right. I want to be marked, taken, claimed by you. Your hands slide from my hair and I stay where I am, standing before you with no shame or fear. Your hands make their way down to mine and you hold them, your fingers pressing tightly into the back of my hands, as your teeth find the first button on your old shirt.

Opening a shirt with your teeth is slower than it is when you use your hands, which is exactly your point. You want me to be frustrated and whining, the kind of impatience that always makes you chuckle. I do my best to stand still while the fabric opens and lets cool air in over me, air that doesn't do the slightest to cool my body. I want you too much. I can already feel the wetness you create in me with just the promise of your touch. Your teeth find the last button and it comes loose under your tongue, right over my belly. You lean forward and press your lips to my tummy, smiling a little when you feel me tremble. Your hands let go of mine and you are on your knees, your fingertips making light trails up my thighs. My legs are smooth and soft from the care I have taken, from the hours I spent preparing my body for your pleasure. You notice and your body responds.

You take your time at first, but impatience makes your hands unsteady and faster. When I can't stand it anymore I let out a deep groan and my hands find your hair. I push you down farther and you go, more than willing. Your hands suddenly find my hips and you pull me to you. The gasp that rips from my throat is nothing compared to the cry of pleasure you pull from me. I feel your tongue gently slide over my neat curls and I know you can taste vanilla. Your tongue slides lower and my knees begin to shake. You hold me up with your broad hands on my pale hips, demanding that I stay there in my place and accept the pleasure you want to give. Your tongue is shockingly hot against my clit, and you moan when you taste me. I know you love this. The fact that I am trembling in your hands is a delicious plus. You move your tongue in circles, then your lips begin to gently suck. You keep it up...and up...and up until I am begging to come. I have the sudden thought that you will keep me upright until I come for you, but you take pity on me. Perhaps it is the fact that my nails are digging into your skin that makes you relinquish your hold on me. I fall to the floor with you, your tongue following my skin and leaving a trail of wetness all the way up to my chin.

And that's how I begin with you, running my tongue from your chin and down. Your t-shirt disappears without a thought. Your jeans open easily under my hands. I push them down while my mouth blazes a trail down your chest. You are already hard and throbbing, and your hands immediately find their way into my hair. I remember how shy you once were and I smile, right before I slide my tongue over your slick head. You groan in the way that is uniquely you, the sound that says, please don't stop, please give me more of that. I swirl my tongue around your head echoing the way used yours on my clit. I wonder if you are aware of the imitation, but I don't care. You buck into me then and your hands push down, and as you slide past my lips you moan at the incredible heat of it.

Your hands leave my hair and you caress my back, lifting the shirt higher off my hips so that you can see the dip in my spine, the curve of my legs. I begin to move up and down on you, letting my lips and tongue and teeth suck you inside my mouth and then push you out. My hands push your jeans farther down. You thrust up into me, wanting as much as I can give you. I can taste the drops of come that flow out of you and into my mouth...you taste sweet and addictive. I know how you would taste when you are covered in my own juices, and I suddenly want you driving into me, hard and fast. But I can't pull myself away from the seductive sweetness you are giving me.

My hands find your balls and you moan. You begin to speak to me, telling me how good it feels, telling me what you want to do to me. You tell me that you want to come. I back off then and you groan in frustration. But I don't want to wait anymore. I *can't* wait anymore.

I push you back onto the carpet. Your chest heaves under my hands. Together we remove the rest of your clothes. The lights from the candles in the room shine on your skin, turning you golden. Your hands find my hips again as I straddle you, but I don't take you into me just yet. I run my wetness over you, make your body even harder with yearning for what is yours. I sit up on you and let you watch as I open your old shirt. The fabric falls open over my breasts and you reach up to touch my nipples gently with your fingers and I let my head fall back. You watch my hair cascade down my shoulders, almost brushing your legs, it has grown so long. I move my hands up to yours and push them down, placing your fingers on my hips.

I touch myself then, my fingers working over my own breasts. One hand slides up my neck and finds my hair, pulling it up to cool my neck, piling it high on my head. My other hand abandons my nipples and slides down my body. I touch you gently before I touch myself. Your eyes watch everything. My finger slides over my clit just as I slide my body over yours. You let out the breath you don't even realize you were holding. I watch your eyes as I take your cock into my body, not hesitating. You are thick enough to stretch me and I moan as I take you in all the way, needing you so badly. You arch into me and hold your body hard against me, letting me move back against you.

I slide up until you are almost out of me, then I slide down again. I take my slow, agonizing time. Each time I move up you watch my juices coat you. I need to come and you can feel it, you can hear it and see it in me, as you always can. You just hold my hips harder and tell me to take what I need, to come for you. Your body is tense and ready and I know what you want. So I rock harder, take your cock deeper. I touch myself again and again and between the two of us, my orgasm hits hard. I come with a shout, a sound that mingles with your voice as you encourage me to keep going, to drive you through it, to make the sensation
all it can possibly be.

Then you move under me, and what I suspected you wanted, you do. You gently lift me off of you and let me tumble gracefully onto my back. Then you are above me, lifting my legs over your shoulders without pause. You don't want to take your time. You don't want to make my body ready or ask me what I want. That isn't what this is about.

You drive into me hard. One thrust, hard and vicious, deep into the core of me. It makes me cry out in pleasure and maybe a little pain. You know that I want anything from you, that I will match you with every thrust, that the thought of saying no will never enter my mind, because you and I are never like that. My hands dig into the carpet. I thrust back up at you until I can't match you anymore, then your body drives into mine with a power that always surprises me. I know I am tight around you, just the way you always like it, and I can feel a mixture of you and me running out of me and onto the carpet below. Your teeth find my neck and sink down. Your hands link with mine. You drive into me, claiming once again what is yours.

I take all of you, every plunge of your cock meeting with a giving softness. I tighten my body around you. I can't move beyond that, I can only tremble under your superior weight as you take me. This is what you want, what I want. I whisper in your ear, make yourself come. Use my body. I am yours. Take me, I am yours. I belong to you. I want to feel you inside, to know that my body had made yours explode in passion. I need that from you. I need to feel like your woman again.

You hold back a little, just to savor the moment. You hold back until the words "I am yours" are firmly embedded in your mind, until my voice chases out all other thought. Only then can you let yourself go, and you do, your body suddenly moves deeper into me. You begin to whimper. I kiss your throat and feel you moan under my lips. I want you to come inside me, to come for me, to share with me that moment when all your defenses are down. I want to feel like you are mine.

You bend lower over me and thrust, hard and steady. My body burns around you and I come again, this time the clenching around your rod drives you past the point of no return. You hold your breath for a long moment as you feel your body build into the feeling, then you come with a shout, a raspy sound that escapes when you let your breath go. You push against me and into me one last time, and I feel your passion inside me, feel your juices splash out into me with a force that is almost painful. You hold me closer for a moment, until your body gives me all you have in you.

Then you gently lower my legs, and you lower yourself to my side. I look at you, let my fingers trace your face as I feel your essence within me. Your shirt is still wrapped around my shoulders. Yet I don't need it to remind me at this moment. I don't need it to remind me, for you have made me feel beautiful and sexy with your words, your body, your heart. I look into your eyes and see only myself reflected there.

That is my fantasy, my darling. Perhaps a simple fantasy, just like this shirt I wear is a simple shirt. But to me it is far from simple. *You* are far from simple.

Tonight as I sit here and dream about you, as I watch the candles burn low and wonder about you, as I hope and pray that you are sleeping well and peacefully with dreams of me....

Tonight, I have never been so much in love. I have never felt such a desire to belong to you, body and soul. I am yours. No matter what happens or what we go through, I am yours. The center of us always comes back to these simple yet complex things...your old shirt draped over my shoulders, my voice in your ear, a connection that cannot be explained by anyone else simply because they can't feel it.

But we can.

ZAMBONI MAN
by Suzanna O'Neil

The pretty brunette walks into the rink, knowing that he is on-site. Excitement rushes through her as she waits for him to look her way. Tonight she has on her favorite black velvet mini skirt with a lace-up design on the front. Her black nylons cover her shapely legs from toe to hip, and her voluptuous breasts glow above the neckline of her low cut T-shirt. A man's white oxford is buttoned in two places at her waist, creating a vision of false modesty. Would anyone guess that she has only a tiny lace thong beneath her velvet skirt?

As she stands behind a crowd of people, she waits for him to notice her. They have a good connection. She knows that he'll feel her watching him in moments, and she's right. Suddenly, he looks over the crowd and sees her waiting by the glass. She stands gazing into the ice rink area at the game in motion. Fans press him with questions, and he can't get away. The path leading to her seems impossible to reach.

Quietly, she slips away, maneuvering through the hustle of people, and opens the doors to the main rink. She begins her walk to the coffee room in the back. She knows he'll follow her.

With the last of the questions finally answered, he veers through the crowd to the spot where she was standing, but she's gone. He quickly looks through the windows and sees her making her way down to the associates' room in the back. He hurries past the Zamboni and toward the coffee room.

When he enters the room, she turns to face him.

"Found you," he says, grinning.

"I knew you would."

He moves closer and they kiss. At 6'5" he towers over her, his arms holding her pressed against him. She looks up to see his eyes flickering from dark hazel to green. God, is he handsome. She's waited so long for this kiss.

It is minutes before his last flooding of the ice. He sits, and she straddles his lap and faces him with her mini-skirt almost exposing what little she has to hide. They kiss as he moves his hands up her sides and slowly brings them forward to touch her firm breasts and stroke her erect nipples. Their kisses grow more intense, the desire undeniable. They could kiss forever.

But they don't have forever.

After a moment, he breaks the kiss. "It's time," he says, motioning to the clock on the wall. They part so that he can ring the bell and hurry these people out to finish his work. As the last of the patrons clears out, they stroll down the rink together, checking the vacant changing rooms that smell of hard bodies. The intoxicating odors of men sweating and working out is overwhelming for her, an unexpected aphrodisiac.

She circles her arms around his neck and begins to kiss him intently. She pushes him toward a nearby bench, and he has no choice but to sit. He opens her shirt, exposing her breasts, thoughts of his work vanishing. Pushing her breasts together, he runs his tongue down between the valley.

"I have to finish," he whispers. "*Then* we'll have time."

Once he had promised her a ride on his Zamboni and tonight's the night to ride. The ice has to be flooded for the morning crew to come in to skate. As they walk to the rear of the building, her mind is full of situational lust. All possible places and positions present themselves.

They open the doors and approach their ride into the iced area. As he removes the water hose, she asks where he wants her to sit.

"On top," he tells her. "Where the steering wheel is."

She gives him a look, then begins to climb onto the Zamboni, trying her best not to expose herself beneath her very short skirt.

She moves on top of the Zamboni and as she lifts herself, he walks around the back, catching a glimpse of the tops of her nylons. Oh, man. He can hardly wait. He'd fuck her right here, if he could. On the ice. Pressing her against the cold metal machine. Taking her fast.

Instead, he climbs onto the Zamboni and turns on the machine. She sits with her ankles crossed at first, but when he speeds up slightly, she feels herself swaying and her legs parting.

"Are you all right?" he asks, slowing down slightly.

"More than all right," she says. Her face is flushed a light shade of red and at every turn the shade gets darker. Her legs work themselves apart and his view becomes more vivid. He smiles when he catches a sight of her peach-colored thong, and she blushes even darker.

"You don't have to be shy," he assures her, realizing this is the most he's enjoyed his work in a long, long time. The ice is almost finished, and he stops the Zamboni. Moving forward on his seat, he urges her to spread her legs apart further.

"Show me," he tells her.

"Show you what?" she's all about teasing him now.

"Your pretty thong. It's lacy, isn't it?"

Gingerly, she spreads her legs, and he traces his index fingers along the edges of the thong, then runs his fingers under the elastic, tugging gently. She lifts her ass to allow the thong to be removed. After placing the lacy fluff in his pocket, he continues.

Her legs now suspend on either side of the steering wheel. He stands and leans toward her, kissing her as his hands run up her stockings. His erection is visible in his tight jeans. She reaches forward, releasing the belt, button and zipper on his Levis. She sighs when she sees how hard he is. But he's not ready for her to touch him yet. He has other plans.

Moving backwards a bit, he uses his fingers to gently open her lips and feel the wetness he has caused. Parting her nether lips, he bends to kiss her pussy. She feels his breath between her thighs as he slowly starts to flicker his tongue against her. He traces slowly up the middle with the tip of his tongue, taunting her. His fingers run up and down her legs, tickling gently. The motion feels so good, she can hardly stand it. Finally, she says, "Wait. Help me down."

He lifts her off the top of the Zamboni, and immediately she tells him to push his seat back as far as he can. His jeans are split open, and she has enough room to maneuver herself on her knees in front of him. She begins licking and sucking on his hard head, slowly lashing at it with her tongue, licking slowly around the crown and then running her tongue down the shaft. She takes him as deep as she can into her mouth and sucks him hard.

"You're going to make me come," he says, his fingers running through her dark hair. She likes that she's gotten to him so quickly, and she would happily drain his every drop, but he pulls her up onto his lap and starts the Zamboni again, his hard-on like glistening steel against his thigh. He drives to the back, dumps the snow, and lowers the door. She climbs off his lap and waits for him.

As he rinses off the blades, she stands behind him. There are very few words. But when he's finished, she grabs his hand and leads him into the walkway to the front of the arena. She looks up at the bleachers and then back at him with a smile, then begins walking up the stairs to the bleachers. He stops her by grabbing her hips. Remembering he has her thong in his pocket, he lifts her skirt exposing her bare buttocks and sex to the coolness of the ice rink. She had told him before that it doesn't get cold beneath her naked skirts. He investigates for himself, and realizes that she's told him the truth. Heat meets his fingertips, and he suddenly has a different idea.

He grabs her and leads to the showers in the Referees' changing room. Slowly removing her clothes, he fondles her breasts and for the first time views her completely naked. She helps him remove his own clothes so that they are equally naked, touching flesh to flesh. There are no secrets, no mysteries left between them. They move toward the shower and he starts up the spray of water.

She enters the shower behind him. He turns to face her, caressing her body with his soft hands, then gently covering her with soap. He runs his hand up her neck, then descends down her chest to her very round, firm breasts. He ventures lower to her stomach, tracing his hand over her smooth skin. He moves closer to her, embracing her in his arms, soaping her back and down to her ass. He gently squeezes it and nibbles on her neck. By now she can feel his hardness against her as he holds her tight and close.

He breaks from her so that he can wash her legs. Slowly he travels up her ankle to her calf and continues to her thigh. She spreads her legs so that he can wash his way closer to her sex, but he stops at the thigh and begins at the ankle of the other leg. He moves a bit faster this time, smelling the sweet scent of her arousal. He smooths the soap between her thighs, starting at the front and slowly gliding his soap covered hand to the back. Then, separating her lips slightly, he begins grazing his finger over her labia and clit. Her body shakes with the gentle sensation. On his knees now exploring her sex, he continues to soap and circle his fingers around her hot mound. Cupping some water in his hands he rinses her off, making sure no traces of soap remain behind as his mouth gets closer and his tongue slides out to stroke her clit.

He is aware that she is totally turned on by what he is doing and forces his fingers into her. She parts her legs even wider to give him better access. As he continues, the need to get inside of her is more and more overwhelming. But now she moves away from him and begins caressing his body with her small hands. Taking the soap, she gently begins to lather him all over. He stands as she begins at his shoulders then ventures lower to his stomach, then she moves downward to his legs, and then between them.

She lathers his shaft and balls. She makes sure the soap is completely rinsed off his shaft and head and gently flows past his balls leaving no traces of soap. Extending her tongue, she licks first at the head, then circles it with her tongue. Cupping his balls, she licks and nibbles her way up his shaft. Then she slowly takes his head in her mouth and sucks hard on it. While grabbing his balls firmly in one hand, she jerks slowly on his shaft with the other. She reaches behind him, running her nails down the back of his legs and grabbing his ass on the way up, pulling him deeper into her mouth. Continuing her sucking motions, she takes his head as deep into her mouth as she can. The constant pressure is building in his balls. He warns her that he's about to come, yet she seems relentless to finish the job.

But he makes her stand and then turns her around. Bending her forward so that his cock is at her entrance, he plunges forward. The heat so intense and the tight feeling around his cock so deliriously good, that he begins to piston himself into her. Her inside muscles clench around his cock as he increases his tempo until he's driving in deep and hard. The sensation is so intense, that she smashes back against him as his balls hit her clit. Her body begins to convulse, and the combination of her shaking body and her tight clenches around his cock, take him over the edge.

They climax together, one urging on the other, until both are shaky with the power of their pleasure. She leans back to into him, his cock still inside her, her hands holding her steady against the cool wall of the shower. He pulls out slowly and turns her around. She tilts her head back to kiss him, as the jets of water flow gently over their bodies. When the water begins to cool, they leave the shower and dry off.

Without a word, they put their clothes back on and slowly leave the room—heading out into the rink again, and from the heat into the cold.

BONUS STORY!

KITCHEN FIRE
by Julia Rebecca

I sat on the kitchen counter, my bare feet dangling beneath my calf-length skirt. You were cleaning the dishes while our significant others stayed on the balcony to finish their drinks and enjoy the evening breeze. This was our typical after-dinner pattern; they stayed out, we went in and I kept you company while you washed up. I sipped my wine and enjoyed the sight of you, tall and broadshouldered, efficiently restoring order to the kitchen.

As you walked toward me to put away the silverware, I mischievously spread my legs, forcing you to stand between them to reach the drawer. Looking into your blue eyes, I smiled a silent dare up at you. You met my flirtatious gaze for a few moments, then glanced behind me toward the balcony. Smiling, you said with mock exasperation, "They're at it again."

Shifting around to follow your gaze, I saw our lovers standing at the balcony railing, entwined in a comfortable embrace. The sight of them together fanned the small flame of desire that is in me when you are near. Turning back to you, I smiled. "That looks like fun." I carefully set my wine glass to one side, then leaned forward and slid my arms around your neck. "Shall we give it a try?"

I watched your face and waited, hoping that you would take me up on my offer. My lover and I had often talked about deepening the intimate friendship we had with the two of you. He had fantasized about watching another man make love to me. I had fantasized about having you while he watched. Opportunities had presented themselves, but we had never dared to follow up on them. This time, my patience was rewarded.

I heard the silverware clatter to the counter then felt your hands on my back as you lowered your head to gently kiss me. My fingers caressed your neck and moved through your soft brown hair as we kissed once, twice, then a third time. Again we kissed; I flicked my tongue across your lips. A small sound escaped from you and you pulled me closer. You licked my lips seeking, and receiving, entry to my mouth. Thought escaped me as your tongue warmed my wine-cooled mouth. I'd kissed you before, but never felt your desire, your forcefulness, in those kisses. Sensation was all as I tasted you, felt your chest against my breasts and your arms firmly holding me. The small flame within me began to burn more brightly. Without conscious thought my legs lifted to your hips and tightened.

The incoherent sound of protest forced from me when you took your mouth from mine was replaced by a moan of pleasure as your lips fastened on my neck. My head fell back as your hot mouth scorched a path down my throat. Legs wrapped around your body I pulled you close, I was on fire.

Heated, agonizing pleasure seared through me as you worked your way down, sucking, licking, sizzling. Dimly, I heard the balcony door open, barely aware of the sound's significance. You reached up, confident, almost impatient, and pulled my dress off my shoulder. Your fiery lips kissed and nibbled their way toward my breast.

The fire within me burned incandescent as you licked your way around my nipple. Leaning back on one hand, the other firmly around your shoulders, I arched my back, offering more of what you had begun to taste. Tantalizing, your tongue circled closer and closer for an eternity until, finally, you sucked my nipple into your mouth. I was gone; fantasy had become reality. I was engulfed in burning desire.

"You know," I heard him say, "she'll come if you keep doing that."

I felt more than heard the moan in your throat. You tongued my nipple harder; you were going to find out if he was right. Forcing my eyes open, I turned my head toward the direction of his voice. They stood there, watching. He held her in front of him, her back against his chest. His hands caressed her breasts; his lips tasted her neck. Mesmerized and aroused, we stared at each other. No shame, no embarrassment; desire fueled desire. Had this been their secret fantasy, too?

You increased your tempo, sucking harder and pressing against me. My head fell back as my pelvis slid forward, heels digging into you, desperate to melt into you. Friction created more heat as, legs spread wide, I rubbed against your burning hardness. The feel of your mouth, the press of your body, our lovers touching watching and aroused - all combined to fuel the inferno within me.

A soft hand touched mine. Firmly in your embrace, I clasped her hand in mine. It was warm, heated by passion. Theirs? Ours? Both.

He whispered, "Let go. Let him take you." My lover's words acted like gasoline applied to fire. The volcano inside me began to erupt. While our lovers watched, I flamed to orgasm in your arms.

About the Authors

Charlie Anders ("Never Miss Your Water") can dance underwater without getting wet. Her first novel, Choir Boy, will be published in March 2005 by Soft Skull Press. Her writing has appeared in Salon.com, Punk Planet, ZYZZYVA, the SF Bay Guardian, Watchword, Kitchen Sink and the anthologies Bottoms Up, It's All Good and Pills, Thrills Chills & Heartache. She's the publisher of other magazine <www.othermag.org>.

Jocelyn Bringas ("Shady Ways") is a 19 year old who enjoys writing and is an ardent Backstreet Boys fan. Her work has appeared in Velvet Heat and Down & Dirty volume 2 (Pretty Things Press). She runs a website: http://allihave.net/delicious/

M. Christian ("Rose's Vibrator") M. Christian is the author of the critically acclaimed and best-selling collections Dirty Words, Speaking Parts, and The Bachelor Machine.   He is the editor of The Burning Pen, Guilty Pleasures, the Best S/M Erotica series, The Mammoth Book of Future Cops and The Mammoth Book of Tales of the Road (with Maxim Jakubowski) and over 14 other anthologies.   His short fiction has appeared in over 150 books including Best American Erotica, Best Gay Erotica, Best Lesbian Erotica, Best Transgendered Erotica, Best Fetish Erotica, Best Bondage Erotica and ... well, you get the idea.   He lives in San Francisco and is only some of what that implies.

Dante Davidson ("Better than Sex") is a tenured professor in Santa Barbara, California. His short stories have appeared in *Bondage* (Masquerade), *Naughty Stories from A to Z* (PTP), and *Best Bondage Erotica* (Cleis), and *Sweet Life* (Cleis). With Alison Tyler, he is the co-author of the best-selling collection of short fiction *Bondage on a Budget* (PTP) and *Secrets for Great Sex After Fifty*.

Trisha Dillon ("When the Cat's Away") is a flight attendant who writes in hotel rooms to entertain herself. If she can entertain other people, as well, she's very pleased.

C.D. Formetta ("Everything That You Want") was born in 1972. In Italy she has published "Il nero che fa tendenza" (Clinamen Editrice). Her stories regularly appear on UP magazine. Currently she's working to a comic strip for the publishing house "Nicola Pesce Editore."

When **Sheri Gilmore** ("Pure Sin") isn't creating romantic sexual fantasies for her readers, she's working as a registered nurse or spending time with her husband and three children. Born and raised in the "Bible Belt," she is frequently introduced as the "Black Sheep" of her family. Her most favorite cities are New Orleans, San Francisco, and New York.

Michelle Houston ("Lust Be a Lady") has five ebooks out from Renaissance E Books, as well as a print omnibus of two of them, and stories in several multiple-author anthologies. You can read more about her, or see more of her writing on her personal website, The Erotic Pen (www.eroticpen.net). She loves to receive email, so drop her a line at thewriter@eroticpen.net

Lynne Jamneck ("Jane Bond—Stirred, Never Shaken") is a writer / photographer from South Africa. Her fiction and non-fiction have appeared in various markets & anthologies including *Best Lesbian Erotica 2003*, *Heat Wave*, *Best Of On Our Backs Vol. 2*, *Naked Erotica*, *H.P. Lovecraft's Magazine of Horror*, *Raging Horrormones* and *Ultimate Lesbian Erotica (2005)*. Her first mystery, *Down The Rabbit Hole* (A Samantha Skellar Mystery) is available from Bella Books (as of 28 February 2005). She is the creator and Editor of *Simulacrum: The Magazine of Speculative Transformation*. www.specficworld.com/ simulacrum.html. She likes vodka over ice, anti-heroes and thinks 'dyke' is the sexiest word in the dictionary. To contact her, email her at lynnejamneck@xtra.co.nz

Marilyn Jaye Lewis' erotic short stories and novellas have been widely anthologized in the United States and Europe. Her erotic romance novels include When Hearts Collide, In the Secret Hours, and When the Night Stood Still. She is the editor of a number of erotic short story anthologies including Stirring Up A Storm (Thunder's Mouth Press 2005). Upcoming novels include Twilight of the Immortal, Killing on Mercy Road, and Freak Parade.

Gwen Masters ("Your Old Shirt") is a twenty-something woman living in the shadow of Music Row. She enjoys guitars, and has a shameless fetish for musicians. She currently has several projects in the works, including "Crossroads," an honest and cutting erotic work focusing on the politics of Nashville's Music Industry.

Lee Minxton ("In Brendan's Room") is the pseudonym of a freelance writer living in northern California. Her erotic fiction has been published in the Blowfish.com enewsletter, and is scheduled to appear on the Good Vibrations website. Someday soon, she hopes to find literary stardom (and a nice Catholic boy who yearns to be bad).

Bill Noble's ("Vicky at the Villarosa") accolades range from reader selection as author of one of the Best American Erotica "Stories of the Decade" and a Pushcart Prize nomination, to the National Looking Glass Award for Poetry. He's longtime fiction editor at www.cleansheets.com (http://www.cleansheets.com) .

Suzanna O'Neil ("Zamboni Man") is a trade professional who delves fearlessly into the seduction and the erotic joys of life. Using a combination of real-life experiences and overwhelming desires, she attempts to depict the things that she has enjoyed or dreamed about in her erotic fantasies. A parent, a scholar and a want-to-be writer, Ms. O'Neil strives to push the boundaries with every story.

Heather Peltier ("Quick Fix") is a San Francisco Bay Area based writer and sex educator. She is currently working on an erotic novel.

Tom Piccirilli ("Dostoyevsky") is the author of thirteen novels including NOVEMBER MOURNS, A CHOIR OF ILL CHILDREN,

THE NIGHT CLASS, and COFFIN BLUES. He's sold over 150 short stories in the horror, mystery, and erotica fields. Learn more about him and his work at www.tompiccirilli.com. You can also feel free to drop him a line at PicSelf1@aol.com.

Lina Pierce ("X-Pose") has a degree in Art and Literature from Brown University. She applies her imagination to furthering the Eros of the sensuous life combined with the cultivation of the higher spirit. This is her first published short story. She can be reached at zakpaperno@comcast.net

Julia Rebecca ("Kitchen Fire") is a writer, artist and sailor who lives with her husband on a small island in the Caribbean. Her stories and poetry have been accepted for publication in Closet Desire IV, Swing! Third Party Sex, Ride 'Em Cowboy, Velvet Heat, Many Joys of Sex Toys, and an as-yet un-named erotic women anthology. Erotic works in progress include short stories, poetry, a novel and herself.

Ayre Riley ("...and Leslie") has written for Down & Dirty and Naughty Stories from A to Z, volume 3 (Pretty Things Press), and slave (Venus). Ms. Riley always heard the lyrics in that silly Grease song as "You're the one that I want; sit on a cornball." And don't try to tell her she's wrong.

After a career as teacher and writer of a successful series of children's books, **Cate Robertson** ("Game Night") turned her attention to literary erotica in 2003. She has published her fiction online at Clean Sheets and Scarlet Letters and in *Naked Erotica*. "Game Night" was inspired by the national obsession with hockey in Canada, where Cate lives with her husband.

Thomas S. Roche's ("Kinsey Six") more than 300 published short stories and 300 published articles have appeared in a wide variety of magazines, anthologies and websites. In addition, his ten published books include His and Hers, two books of erotica co-authored with Alison Tyler, as well as three volumes of the Noirotica series. He has recently taken up erotic photography, which he showcases at his website, www.skidroche.com. After a lucky thirteen years in San Francisco, he recently relocated to New Orleans.

Jacqueline Sinclaire ("Options") is a writer by profession but erotic by nature. A firm believer that sex & masturbation is both healthy and necessary, she considers it her civic duty to write smut.

Savannah Stephens Smith ("Call Me Jenny") has a degree in Anthropology, and is a secretary by day and writer by night (and occasionally during her lunch hour). Life doesn't always turn out like one plans. Her work has appeared online at Clean Sheets, Scarlet Letters and other web destinations, as well as in print anthologies. She finds it hard to resist chocolate, good whiskey and buying more books. She struggles to quit smoking, but can't resist smouldering a little.

Alison Tyler ("Four on the Floor") is a shy girl with a dirty mind. Over the past decade, she has written more than 15 naughty novels including *Strictly Confidential*, *Sticky Fingers*, and *Something About Workmen* (all published by Black Lace), and *Rumours* (Cheek). She is the editor of *Batteries Not Included* (Diva); *Heat Wave*, *Best Bondage Erotica 1 & 2*, *Three-Way*, and the upcoming *Heat Wave 2* (all from Cleis Press); and the *Naughty Stories* series, the *Down & Dirty* series, *Naked Erotica*, and *Juicy Erotica* (all from Pretty Things Press). She lives in California. although she retains remnants of a Philly accent.

Sage Vivant ("Unleashed") operates Custom Erotica Source (www.customeroticasource.com), writing tailor-made erotic fiction for individual clients. Her stories have appeared in numerous anthologies, from *Best Women's Erotica* to *Naughty Stories 2* and *3*. She is the author of *29 Ways to Write Great Erotica* (available at her Web site), and the editor of *Swing!* With M. Christian, she is the co-editor of *The Best of Both Worlds: Bisexual Erotica* and the upcoming *Confessions: Admissions of Sexual Guilt*.